SKYWAKE
INVASION

JAMIE RUSSELL

WALKER
BOOKS

First published 2021 by Walker Books Ltd
87 Vauxhall Walk, London SE11 5HJ

2 4 6 8 10 9 7 5 3 1

Text © 2021 Jamie Russell
Cover illustration © 2021 Matt Griffin

The right of Jamie Russell to be identified as author of this
work has been asserted by him in accordance with the
Copyright, Designs and Patents Act 1988

This book has been typeset in Berkeley Oldstyle

Printed and bound by CPI Group (UK) Ltd, Croydon CR0 4YY

British Library Cataloguing in Publication Data:
a catalogue record for this book is available from the British Library

ISBN 978-1-4063-9751-2

www.walker.co.uk

For Isobel and Alice,
my favourite co-op partners

0

MAKE MINE A SKINNY
LATTE ... TO GO

Right after she fired it, the alien plasma rifle glowed in Casey's hands. It was big. It was heavy. Most of all, though, it was hot. It crackled with a tingling, electrical heat that made the hairs on the backs of her hands stand to attention like soldiers on parade.

She looked at the hole she'd just blasted in the side of Starbucks. A perfect circle, like when she used a pencil and compass in Mr Donovan's maths class. She could see right through it into the pizza restaurant next door. The remaining bricks, sliced in half by the plasma rifle's searing blast, burned red like charcoal in a barbecue. Wisps of black smoke curled above what was left of the baristas' station.

A hulking alien soldier stood beside the hole. It wore heavy, black armour and a curved metal helmet that obscured its face. Two blood-red mechanical eyes were set in the helmet. They stared at her angrily.

If she'd been a little more accurate, the hole would have been smack bang in the middle of the alien's armoured chest.

But you weren't accurate, Casey thought to herself. *You totally choked.*

It was true. The minute she'd picked up the plasma rifle, her body had flooded with fear and adrenaline. She'd pulled the trigger too early and the heavy weapon had jerked out of her hands. Her shot – the shot that was going to save her life – had gone wide and destroyed the wall instead.

And that was why she was now standing in a ruined Starbucks being eyeballed by an alien soldier. This thing had travelled thousands of light years from some distant corner of interstellar space to invade Earth and had almost been taken out by a fifteen-year-old girl.

She guessed it wasn't very happy.

"Um…" Casey muttered, letting the hand holding the rifle drop to her side. She desperately wanted to say some last words before she was vaporized. But her mind had gone blank. The only thing she could think of was a four-letter word. She didn't want that on her gravestone.

The alien filled the silence himself. She decided it was a "him", even though she couldn't actually see who, or what, was inside the bulky combat suit.

"*Rth'he calfu mort,*" he said in a mechanical voice. The tone sounded insulting, like he was saying, *You should have aimed better, you stupid girl.*

"Yeah." Casey grimaced. "I guess you're right."

The alien raised his plasma rifle. It hummed in his large hands. Casey stared down the barrel. It was as black as death. She knew he wouldn't choke.

She closed her eyes and swore under her breath. *If the alien dude can't speak English,* she decided, *then it probably doesn't count...*

1

IRL – IN REAL LIFE

Casey hadn't woken up that morning expecting to die, but she had been ready to kill. Her younger brother, Pete, had stormed into her room while she was still asleep, ignoring the sign on her door that clearly said: WARNING: NO STUPID PEOPLE BEYOND THIS POINT. He jumped on her bed, making the mattress bounce up and down like a dinghy in rough seas.

"Casey, wake up! The tournament's all over the news!" he yelled. "They said it's happening in other cities too: New York, Madrid, Johannesburg, Seoul and that one in the Middle East with the enormous skyscrapers."

Casey cracked open a single, sleep-encrusted eye and glared at him. Pete was compact and wiry with a mop of shaggy black hair. At eleven he was four years younger than her and he had been born prematurely, making him small for his age. But what he lacked in size he made up for in excitability.

"What time is it?" Casey asked. Her mouth felt dry and scratchy.

"I don't know. Probably about six."

She groaned and tried to pull the duvet over her head. It only came up as far as her nose because Pete was weighing it down. She lay back and glared at him over the covers.

"They had a special segment about eSports on the local news," he continued. "The presenters were totally clueless. But they showed some *SkyWake* footage *and* they interviewed Xander Kane. You know, the pro-player who makes all those YouTube videos?"

Casey knew who Xander Kane was. Pete was obsessed with him.

"Why are you up so early?" she demanded. "You never get up at six. Not even at Christmas."

"I couldn't sleep," Pete told her. "I kept dreaming I was hiding in the vents on the dropship map. I was the last man standing and all I had was a psi grenade. Just as they found me, I woke up. Anyway, come on. We've got to get over there."

"There's no rush," she yawned. "The tournament doesn't start for hours." Her hair, which she'd recently dyed with blue streaks in the same style as her favourite gaming YouTuber, was a tangled mess. She stuck out her bottom lip and blew some sky-coloured strands out of her face.

"But people are already queuing up," Pete said, bouncing off the bed in a wild flurry of limbs. "There'll be over two hundred players in London alone."

"Oh yeah? But how many good ones?" Casey asked.

"None as good as you," Pete said. And he meant it.

"Shame I'm not competing, then," Casey replied, swinging her legs out of bed and heading for the door. Pete followed her.

"Wait, *what?* Why not? They sent you a VIP invite and everything!"

"Because if I meet my team, they'll find out who I really am."

"They already know who you are. You're Casey Flow," he said, using her gamertag: **CASEY_FLOW.** "The best *SkyWake* player I've ever seen."

"Yeah, but here's the thing. They all think Casey Flow is a boy."

For the first time that morning, Pete was lost for words. He stood there on the landing, trying to process what his sister had just said. Casey shut the bathroom door in his face.

"Well, today's going to be *really* interesting," he muttered to himself.

SkyWake – always one word, always a capital "S" and "W" – was the gaming phenomenon of the year. The online team shooter had arrived out of nowhere back in January as a free-to-play download. By February, it had hit twenty million players worldwide. It kept on growing month after month and its mysterious developers, Area 51, had reputedly made millions from merchandise sales alone.

Casey had been playing since the start, and like her brother she had even begun to dream about it. She could draw each of the game's maps – the beach assault, the weapons factory, the dropship and the alien city – from memory. There was something incredibly immersive about the game's level design.

The invitation from Area 51 had arrived a week ago, pinging into her inbox from out of the blue. The highest-ranked teams in the UK were being invited to take part in a global eSports tournament to find *SkyWake*'s best of the best. Casey's team was among those picked to compete.

Over breakfast, as her mum buzzed around her getting ready to leave for work, Casey watched the news on TV. Footage from *SkyWake* flashed up on-screen.

"I wish you wouldn't waste your time on these silly games," her mum complained as she filled a travel mug with coffee. She was always a little testy when she had to work a Saturday shift. "All that shooting and killing isn't good for you." She smoothed down her nurse's uniform and then gave Casey one of her serious stares. "Plus, I don't want you meeting people you've been talking to online."

"We're just going to look around," Casey assured her. "We're not meeting anyone. We're not even going to play."

Pete looked sideways at her, uncertain whether she was telling the truth or not.

"Are any of your friends going?" her mum asked.

Casey shook her head. None of her friends were big gamers. But Pete was. At least she'd have some company if he tagged along. Mum snapped the lid shut on her mug and glanced at the clock.

"Just make sure you stay together," she told Casey firmly. "Pete's your responsibility. I'm trusting you to keep him safe."

"Why is she always in charge?" Pete moaned, slipping his cereal bowl into the sink. "Just because she's old enough to have a phone and dye her hair silly colours."

"It's one colour," Casey said sharply. "Bubblegum Blue."

Pete snorted in derision. "It makes you look like an anime character."

Their mum glanced at the clock again. She looked tired and pale. Casey suddenly felt sorry for her.

"At least her hair will make her easy to spot in the crowd," she told Pete, kissing him goodbye. She winked at Casey and then hurried out of the door. By the time Casey noticed she'd forgotten her coffee, it was too late to go after her.

Later that morning, Casey sat on the bus twiddling the army dog tags she always wore round her neck. They had belonged to her dad, an officer in the Royal Engineers. She'd started wearing them as a necklace after he'd died. She liked to let her fingers run over the letters that spelled out his full name: *Michael Charles Henderson*.

She sensed Pete watching her.

"What are you thinking about?" he demanded.

"I was just wondering what Dad would have thought about *SkyWake*," Casey said, slipping the dog tags back under her hoodie. "I think he'd have loved it. It's as if it was made for him."

Their dad had been an avid video-game player and collector. He'd taught Casey and Pete everything he knew about games, from *Pac-Man* to *Halo*. Which was a lot.

Pete scowled. He didn't like talking about their dad. He still missed him so much, and if he was truthful, he was jealous that his sister had spent more time with him in the weeks before he died than he had.

"Well, *I* wonder what he'd think about you lying to your team," Pete replied. "Good leaders are supposed to be honest with their squads. I don't get why you didn't just tell them you were a girl."

Casey sighed and turned to face him. "Boys can freak out when they hear a girl in team chat," she explained. "All I have to do is say, *We're getting flanked,* or, *I need healing,* and they go, *OMG! Are you a gurrrrl?* and, *You suck. Go and play with your Barbies!*"

"Boys really say that to you?" Pete asked, shocked and annoyed on her behalf.

"Only some of them. But the sexist ones are usually the loudest."

"Well –" he shrugged – "I guess that's why the game has a mute button. If you don't like what they're saying, just block them."

"But *SkyWake* is a team shooter," Casey snapped, exasperated. "If you mute everyone, you can't work together. And if you can't work together, you can't win. I was just playing about with a voice changer when I realized everyone acted different when they thought I was a boy. So I kept using it. People always assume Casey is a boy's name anyway."

"So no one on your team knows you're a girl?"

Casey shook her head. She'd started using the voice changer before she met the players who'd become her *SkyWake* clan, so they'd only ever known her as a boy. It seemed silly now. Her teammates were good guys, but by the time she realized that, it was too late to tell them the truth without making it into a big drama. She'd never expected to meet them, but then the invites arrived for a gaming tournament in London. In real life.

And IRL there is nowhere to hide.

2

TRICK OF THE LIGHT

The West Point shopping centre was the biggest indoor mall in Europe. Spread over eight floors, it had chain restaurants and pop-up food stalls, a cinema, a skating rink, a gym and even an indoor garden with real plants. It would take three hours to walk around the whole of it ... longer if you actually stopped in any of the hundreds of shops.

Today was busier than usual, as the Saturday crowds were joined by hundreds of *SkyWake* fans arriving for the tournament. Several TV news vans, easy to spot because of the satellite dishes on their roofs, were parked in the restricted area of the outdoor car park. Reporters and their camera operators stood near by, broadcasting live. Casey was excited to recognize a couple of them from TV. They seemed a lot shorter in the flesh.

"Look at all these people," Pete whispered in amazement, pushing through the crowd with Casey trailing behind, struggling to keep up. He was so small and wiry he could scoot through the gaps between the adults with ease.

Casey looked up at the shopping centre as they approached. It had so many floors it made her neck hurt. Up on the roof were a bunch of mobile phone masts and three banks of black solar panels. The company that owned the building had recently announced that it was going carbon-neutral.

It was while Casey was staring at the panels that she saw something odd. She wasn't sure if it was a shimmer or a glimmer. Or maybe a ripple. But whatever it was, it caught her eye.

"Did you see that?" she asked. But her brother had gone on ahead. Casey stopped and looked up again, ignoring the impatient shoppers jostling around her in both directions. The same strange ripple moved across the rooftop. It was as though something was deflecting the light, bending it in unexpected directions. For a moment, she thought she glimpsed the outline of something vast and curved. It dazzled her eyes a little, like sunlight reflecting off a lake.

When she blinked, it vanished.

As she stepped backwards to get a better view, she bumped into a man carrying a cardboard tray of takeaway coffees. Milky suds splashed over his olive-green polo shirt.

"I'm so sorry!" she said, expecting him to be mad. To her surprise, he ignored the mess.

"Did you see something up there?" he asked in a deep, gravelly voice. He had salt-and-pepper hair that was shaved close to his skull in a buzz cut. A purple birth mark, or perhaps a scar, stretched up his neck. The way he stood, stomach in and back straight, was familiar. It was what her dad used to call a "military bearing".

"I thought I did," Casey replied. She glanced at the roof again. There was nothing to see now. "It's like there was something moving up there, on top of the building."

"The reflection off the solar panels does that sometimes," the man told her, shielding his eyes with his free hand as he scrutinized the roof. "It's like a heat haze in the desert. It can make you see things that aren't there. But it's really just a trick of the light."

Casey stared at him, uncertain why he was telling her all this. Then she looked back at the crowd. Pete was almost at the main entrance.

"I have to go," she said. "I'm really sorry about spilling your coffee."

The buzz-cut man ignored her, still staring up at the rooftop.

Casey left him to it and joined the sea of people heading towards the main entrance, where a couple of stressed-out security guards were trying to maintain order. They were clearly overwhelmed by the size of the crowds.

Before she went inside, she looked over her shoulder to see if the man was still there. He was walking towards a black minivan, carrying his soggy tray of coffees. As he approached the vehicle, its rear doors opened. Inside, Casey glimpsed a man and a woman sitting in front of a bank of computer equipment. They were crumpled and sweaty and the man needed a shave. They looked like they'd been in there for a while.

Casey wondered if they were a news crew, although their van didn't have a TV station logo on it. The buzz-cut man climbed in and the van doors slammed shut.

Something about it made Casey feel uneasy. She looked around for Pete, remembering her mum's instructions. Whatever happened today, she wasn't going to let her little brother out of her sight.

*   *   *

The *SkyWake* tournament was happening on the first floor. At the top of the escalators, Casey and Pete were greeted by a giant alien hanging from the ceiling. Its squid-like tentacles stretched out in every direction. A few confused-looking shoppers stood underneath it, staring up at its enormous, bulbous head. They clearly had no idea what it was. That was the thing about video games. Most adults didn't know anything about them.

"This. Is. Amazing," Pete whispered under his breath. The alien was one of the Bactu, an ancient race of extra-terrestrials. They were one of *SkyWake*'s two main factions. Pete reached out to touch the dangling tentacles. He wasn't quite tall enough.

Casey headed over to the sports hall where the eSports arena had been set up. The entrance had been dressed to resemble a military checkpoint. Sandbags were piled high on either side of the doorway with black camouflage netting strung over the top. A long line of gamers queued to get inside while a bored-looking young woman in a *SkyWake* T-shirt checked their invitations on her tablet.

Behind her stood two hulking Arcturian soldiers, the sworn enemy of the Bactu. They wore black armour and carried enormous plasma rifles in their gloved hands. Their mechanical eyes, set deep in their their helmets, burned red.

"Look at those outfits," Pete whispered, staring at the soldiers in awe as he caught up with his sister.

"They must be professional cosplayers," Casey said, admiring the level of detail on their suits. She wondered how the costume designers had managed to mimic the fiery gaze that gave the Arcturians their "Red Eye" nickname.

Her phone buzzed.

"Who is it?" Pete asked, straining to see the screen as she read the message.

"It's Cheeze."

CH33ZEMUNK3Y was one of the players in her online clan.

"Cheese? Like cheddar?"

"No, like *cheezing*. When you exploit a glitch in a game."

"Don't you know his real name?"

Casey shook her head. "I don't know any of their names. Just their gamertags." Her face clouded as she read the message. "He says they're waiting for me in Starbucks."

"Let's get over there, then."

She pulled him back. "No. I don't want to meet

them. We're just going to watch."

"But they're expecting you!"

"They're expecting a guy," Casey replied. Saying it out loud, it all seemed so stupid. She wished she'd never pretended she was anyone other than herself. "They're going to be mad if they find out I've been lying to them all this time."

The queue moved forward.

"Name?" asked the bored-looking woman in a tone that sounded like it was the nine-hundredth time that day she'd asked the same question.

"Casey Henderson. My gamertag is Casey Flow."

The woman arched her eyebrows slightly and scrolled through her list.

"Have you got your VIP invite?"

Casey took out her phone and pulled up the invitation she'd received. The woman scanned the QR code embedded in it and her tablet beeped.

"Clan name?"

"Ghost Reapers. This is my brother. He's my plus one," she added, gesturing towards Pete, who was still staring at the Red Eye cosplayers. He reached out a hand to touch one of them and then jumped in fright when the soldier spun around and pointed his plasma rifle at him.

"Ignore those idiots," the woman said, exasperated. "I've been trying to get them to talk all morning, but they must be method actors or something. They're staying totally in character." She rolled her eyes and handed Casey two plastic badges hanging on blue lanyards. "Your passes."

Casey's badge was stamped with a QR code along with the word **COMPETITOR** in blocky, futuristic writing. Pete's badge was blank with **SPECTATOR** stamped on it. Both were branded with the familiar *SkyWake* logo, two fiery suns rising above the horizon of an alien planet.

Casey slipped her lanyard around her neck.

"Can you tell me something?" she asked the woman. "What happens if a team captain doesn't play? Do you disqualify the whole team or just the captain? Could someone else take my place?"

The woman stared at Casey as if she was talking a foreign language.

"I'm just paid to work here today, hon." She shrugged. "If you want answers, talk to Lee over there. He's in charge." She pointed towards a man who was pacing up and down, having a heated argument with someone on his phone.

"I never ordered any cosplayers," Casey overheard

him saying crossly. "Fine. Well, just don't try and bill me for them later. I'll be checking the invoices."

Casey turned back to quiz the woman some more, but she was already waving a new gamer forwards with a shout of, "Next!"

Casey and Pete stepped aside. Casey's phone buzzed. Cheeze again.

Casey! Where r u?!

"What are you going to do?" Pete asked.

"I don't know," Casey muttered, pocketing her phone and pulling the sleeves of her hoodie down over her hands. She'd got herself into a right mess. What had she been thinking?

"They won't care who you are," Pete reassured her, "just how well you play."

Casey bit her lip. "Maybe if I don't show up they'll find a replacement for me," she suggested doubtfully. She knew that wouldn't be possible. Not this close to the start.

They were just a few metres away from the coffee shop. She stared at the familiar logo. Pete followed her gaze and smiled slyly to himself.

"Oh well," he said, "it's probably better if we don't go. Mum's always warning us about people you meet online. They could be serial killers or anything."

"I guess we could just go and see what they look like…" Casey said. Pete grinned. "But we won't introduce ourselves," she added firmly. "They won't even know who we are unless we tell them. They've never seen either of us before."

"We'll be like spies," Pete said, his imagination running away with him. "Or undercover cops."

"Whatever happens," Casey warned her little brother, "don't give me away."

"Promise," he told her, his face suddenly serious.

In the months since *SkyWake*'s first release, Casey had spent hours leading her team on the battlefield. Shoulder to shoulder, they had fought against the Bactu hordes. Together they had celebrated wild victories and tasted the bitterness of defeat. Through it all they had been a team, a unit, a band of brothers (and one secret sister).

Now, though, as she stood in the doorway of the crowded coffee shop, she realized that she didn't have a clue what any of them looked like. It didn't help that everyone in the coffee shop seemed to be wearing *SkyWake* merch. Everywhere she turned, she saw T-shirts and caps and messenger bags, all emblazoned with the game's logo. She noticed there were plenty of cool-looking gamer girls among the crowd too. Casey bet they didn't use voice changers.

She scanned the faces of the customers, trying to match them to the voices she knew so well. But it was impossible.

"You know," Pete said in a low voice, as she checked out the customers, "maybe you're the one making assumptions."

"What do you mean?"

"Maybe they've been trolling you. Maybe they all use voice changers too. Maybe the whole team are girls!"

For the first time that morning, Casey laughed.

"Don't you know anything about them?" Pete asked.

"I know Cheeze lives in Birmingham – he's good with computers. Fish is from Glasgow – he's always in a bad mood but he's the best tank player I've ever seen. Elite is from London – he wants to be a rapper and keeps getting mugged on the bus. Spock's Brain is from Leeds and—"

"Wait," interrupted Pete. "Whose brain?"

"Spock," Casey said, "like Mr Spock from *Star Trek*. He's a big sci-fi nerd."

"Is that it? Don't you know anything else about them?"

"I know they all love *SkyWake*."

"Look around," Pete told her. "This is *SkyWake* Central."

Her phone buzzed again, insistent.

Casey???!!!!!! Why aren't you answering me???

"Give it to me," said Pete, snatching it from her. "I'll message him."

"Don't you dare!" Casey warned, trying to grab the phone. Pete dodged her, his fingers already typing a message on the screen.

"I'll say you're stuck in traffic and we'll see whose phone buzzes when I reply. Then at least you'll know what they look like…"

"Just give me the phone!" Casey hissed. Her fury stopped Pete in his tracks.

"Fine," he said sulkily, a little hurt. "I was just trying to help."

He was about to pass her the handset when it burst into life with an incoming call.

BRRRRRRRIIIINNNNGGGG!

The ringtone was so loud that several people stopped talking and looked over. Pete fumbled with the phone, trying to mute it.

It was too late. They'd been spotted.

"Casey!" a voice shouted. It belonged to a boy

in a lime-green wheelchair wearing a skateboarder hoodie and holding a phone to his ear. He rolled over to them, propelling himself with his hands, on which he wore fingerless, black leather gloves. Casey saw that his wheelchair was covered in pouches holding a laptop, cables and an electrical toolkit. It looked like a mobile computer repair shop.

"We've been looking for you everywhere!" the boy said, excited. "I'm Cheeze."

Casey was about to reply when she realized that he wasn't talking to her. He was looking directly at Pete.

"You *are* Casey Flow, aren't you?" Cheeze asked, sensing his hesitation.

For an awkward moment nobody said anything. Then a voice spoke.

"Yes, I'm Casey," it said.

But it wasn't Casey who was speaking – it was Pete.

And for some reason, Casey didn't do anything to stop him.

3

DEEP-FRIED MARS BARS

The rest of the Ghost Reapers were sitting in a booth at the back of the coffee shop. Cheeze led Pete over to them. Casey trailed behind.

"Look who I found," Cheeze announced, grabbing Pete by the wrist and holding his arm aloft. "It's our fearless team leader."

The group regarded Pete with inquisitive but welcoming eyes.

"Hey, Casey. Great to finally meet you," said one of the boys. As they introduced themselves, Casey put faces to their gamertags. They were nothing like she had imagined.

XxxEL1TESN1P3RxxX was a pale, wiry boy from Lewisham in South London. He wore a zip-up Puma tracksuit and a pair of brilliant white trainers that looked like they were straight out of the box. He was the team's sniper and, like all snipers, he was convinced he was God's gift to video games.

"Yo. Call me Elite," he said, giving Pete a homie handshake that totally confused him. Pete was so thrown that he even bungled the fist bump at the end.

"Aw-right?" growled **FISH_HEAD_04**, a stocky Scottish boy in a faded *SkyWake* T-shirt. A splodge of dark brown freckles across the bridge of his nose made him look like he'd dunked his face in a jar of Marmite. Casey knew his family ran a fish and chip shop in Glasgow, which explained his gamertag and his accent. He played as the team's tank.

SPOCK5_BR@IN was black and, at seventeen years old, the elder statesman of the group. He had thick glasses that made his serious eyes look like dinner plates. He was planning to study applied mathematics at Oxford University. Casey didn't know what applied mathematics was exactly, but you clearly needed to be super smart to understand it. He played as the team's medic.

"Who's the blue girl?" Fish asked Pete, casting an unimpressed glance at Casey's hair with its streaks of bubblegum dye.

"Um, this is my sister…" stammered Pete. "She's just here to watch."

"I thought you had a brother," Cheeze said, confused.

"Yeah, that's right. A younger brother and an older sister," Pete lied, glancing at Casey nervously.

"Hey," Casey said to the group. She lifted her hand in a pointless wave and instantly regretted it. *Nice one, loser,* she thought to herself.

"Does your sister have a name?" Cheeze asked. He smiled at Casey, trying to put her at ease.

Casey shifted her weight from one foot to the other. This was her moment to tell them the truth. She paused, uncertain where to start. It felt ridiculous now. Why on earth had she kept up the pretence for so long? They stared at her expectantly.

"I'm Rebecca," Casey heard herself say. Rebecca was her mum's name.

The boys, oblivious to her inner turmoil, smiled and nodded politely. Then they turned their attention back to Pete.

"So, team leader," Cheeze asked him, "what's our strategy?"

"I can't believe they think you're me," Casey hissed at Pete later, as they stood outside the tournament zone. The rest of the team were glued to a giant TV screen that was showing *SkyWake* footage on a never-ending loop. They were arguing over which gun was the most over-powered.

"You've been pretending to be a boy all year," Pete snapped back. "It's not my fault you were so convincing."

Casey sighed. It *was* her fault. If she hadn't used a voice changer, nobody would ever have mistaken Pete for their team leader. She was regretting her decision to bend the truth. Pete, however, was loving every minute of it. He'd always wanted to be like Casey, and now here he was with a group of older boys being treated like a star player. He hadn't stopped grinning since this whole mess had started.

Casey didn't know if he would still be grinning when it was time to play in the tournament, though. Pete wasn't bad at *SkyWake*. But he wasn't great either. He didn't play with a proper clan, just with his mates from school. She felt a sinking feeling in her stomach. Could Pete really step into her shoes in more than just name?

This whole thing had become a disaster. The longer the lie went on, the harder it became to tell everyone the truth. It was like a boulder rolling downhill, getting faster and faster. The only way to stop it was by jumping in front of it. But if she did that, it would flatten her...

As the boys continued their argument about which of *SkyWake*'s weapons needed to be nerfed, Cheeze spun around in his wheelchair. He tilted onto his back wheels and then set it back down in front of Casey with a flourish.

"So, Rebecca," he asked casually, "are you a gamer?"

"I bet she's into *Candy Crush*," Fish muttered scornfully. He took a bite from a greasy burger he'd just bought from a food stand.

"I play *SkyWake*, actually," Casey replied. "I love the adrenaline rush you get from first-person shooters."

"What class do you play?" Cheeze asked.

"I bet she's a medic," Fish suggested, taking another bite of burger. "Girls always play support roles. They like helping people. It's in their nature."

"She probably shoots better than you," Cheeze said.

"That wouldn't be hard," Elite chipped in with a grin.

The Scottish boy glared at him. "I don't do guns. I'm a shield tank. It's my job to keep you all alive."

"Is that why you always blame everyone else when we lose?"

"I just call it how I see it, pal!" Fish shot back.

"I main-assault actually," Casey interrupted, her voice as sharp as vinegar. "I like raining down fire on the enemy." She mimed mowing down bad guys. "My dad was in the army…"

"Yeah, your brother told us," Cheeze said. Then he added softly, "He died, didn't he?"

Casey paused a moment, remembering how much she'd told these boys in game chat over the last year. They knew everything about her. Well, almost everything. She felt a little sad. If only she'd been brave enough to be herself, this meet-up could have been fun.

"Who your dad was doesn't have nothing to do with how you play," Fish butted in. "Games aren't like real life."

"I wish they were," Cheeze said. "I'd go around smashing crates looking for loot."

"Yeah? Well, I'd munch a green Mario 'shroom and grow three times my size," Fish said. "Crush all the noobs under my feet."

"If you keep eating junk food, you won't need a mushroom," Brain said, pointing to what was left of Fish's burger. "Do you know how many calories are in that thing? Six hundred and fifty-seven."

"I eat what I want and never put on weight. It's

my superpower," Fish declared through a mouthful of sesame bun.

"That is totally illogical!"

Fish took an extra big bite of his burger, licking ketchup and mayo off his lips. "You can keep your logic, pal," he retorted. "All that maths is turning you into a robot."

Casey smiled to herself. They were always bickering like this in online team chat.

"Next he'll be offering you a deep-fried Mars bar," she said to Brain with a chuckle.

A few weeks back, Fish had told them how his dad put chocolate bars into the deep fat fryer in his family's fish and chip shop. He claimed it was a speciality. Casey was pretty sure he'd said it just to wind Brain up. The older boy was a vegan and he hated junk food with a passion.

Casey, still laughing to herself, looked up, then froze. They were all staring at her in surprise.

"How do you know about that?" Fish demanded, his eyes narrowing.

"Oh, er... Well, I remember Pe— I mean, Casey, telling me." She turned to Pete for help, but he wasn't listening. He was still glued to the *SkyWake* footage on the TV.

"What's up?" he asked, noticing them all looking at him.

"We were talking about the chip shop," Casey said, giving him a hard stare. "The one Fish lives above." She spoke each word with emphasis, trying to get Pete to understand. It didn't work.

"You live above a fish and chip shop?" Pete squealed. "That is so cool! Do you get free chips?"

The rest of the team looked at one another, confused.

"You already know that, Casey," Brain said, his serious eyes squinting behind his spectacles. "We've talked about it loads in game chat."

"Oh yeah," Pete replied hastily, realizing his mistake. "I was just messing with you. Of course I know about it. Everyone does…"

"Even your sister," Fish said. He shot Casey a suspicious look. She could see that he sensed something was wrong but he couldn't quite put his finger on what it was. "You know," he said, turning to Pete, "your voice sounds different in real life."

"Yeah," agreed Elite, "you're a total squeaker, bruv."

"It must be my rubbish mic," Pete lied. "It's only a cheap one."

"You're shorter than I imagined, too," Fish said,

looking him up and down. Just then, an announcement rang out on the public address system.

"Calling all *SkyWake* competitors. We are ready to battle."

In a flash, the boys forgot about interrogating Pete and hurried towards the sandbagged entrance to the tournament zone.

Before Casey could follow, Brain tapped her arm.

"You and your brother need to swap badges. You've got them the wrong way round." He pointed to the COMPETITOR badge that hung around her neck.

Casey nodded and pulled it off, feeling her face redden. Brain was always so smart. She handed the badge to Pete, muttering, "Here you go, *Casey*." She stared at the word SPECTATOR on Pete's badge a moment, then hung it around her neck.

It felt like part of her was dying inside.

"That's better," Brain said, peering at Casey through his thick lenses quizzically. "Isn't it?"

4

THERE'S NO "I" IN TEAM

A few hours later, standing in the spectator area of the tournament zone, Casey was in the depths of despair. Watching the Ghost Reapers step onto the main stage in the centre of the hall, she realized she'd made a terrible mistake. She turned her dad's dog tags over in her hand like worry beads.

The eSports competition had been running all morning and the Ghost Reapers were one of the last teams to play before the break for lunch. The original fifty teams were being slowly whittled down to twenty-five in a series of tense elimination rounds. Casey had watched the clans battle it out one by one, enjoying every minute of it.

When the Ghost Reapers' turn came, though, her heart sank again. She watched nervously as Pete clambered onto the stage and slipped into a high-backed gaming chair in front of a monitor marked CASEY FLOW.

On the main stage were two long tables of monitors and keyboards where the teams sat down to play. Above them hung four jumbo LED TV screens to broadcast the match to the watching spectators.

There was a crackle of anticipation in the air as the Ghost Reapers took their seats. The rumour was that, after lunch, the winning UK teams would face off against the champions from the other shopping centres around the world.

Pete adjusted the monitor. He was so small that one of the stewards had to come over and raise the chair for him. Even the headset was too big for him. Casey felt as though she was watching the build-up to a car crash. Deep down, she knew there was no way her brother would be able to lead her team to victory.

Her heart sank even further when the Ghost Reapers' opponents arrived from the other side of the tournament zone. The enemy team was Strike Force, led by Xander Kane. They strutted onto the stage wearing custom-made black jerseys branded with their clan name and a white and red logo of a fist clenched around a bloody heart.

Xander, the team captain, was a legend in the *SkyWake* community. He was a brilliant player who'd set up the first dedicated streaming channel for the game. Mainly, Casey suspected, so he could show off.

He bounced across the stage, pushing his long, floppy fringe out of his face.

"Xander! Xander!" the arena chanted.

The teenager crossed his index fingers in front of him to form an "X". It was his signature move.

Lee, the man running the event, appeared on the stage. He was the perfect master of ceremonies, brash and loud with the patter of a used-car salesman. His sharp suit glittered under the bright lights.

"This is it, everyone," he said into his radio mic. "The final match of the knock-out rounds. Are you ready?"

The crowd, already hyped up, erupted with excitement.

"We've definitely saved the best for last," he continued, dropping his voice to a stage whisper as if he was letting everyone in on a secret. "Team A is The Ghost Reapers led by Casey Flow. Let's give them a warm welcome…" Pete's face appeared on the jumbo screens, high above the spectators. He gave the camera a dorky thumbs-up. The crowd clapped politely.

"Team B is Strike Force. Led by the one, the only … XANDER KANE!"

There was a thunderclap in the arena.

"XANDER! XANDER! XANDER!" the crowd shouted. Up onstage, the Ghost Reapers looked as if they'd already lost. It was pretty obvious who were the favourites. The boys exchanged worried glances.

"Let's be logical about this," Brain told his teammates through his headset microphone. "Don't get tilted. Work as a team. Calm and methodical. Right, Casey?"

Pete, unused to being called Casey, didn't answer.

"I've got your backs," Elite cackled over the comms channel. "Five headshots in the first thirty seconds. We're gonna be munching calamari tonight." Then he burst into a rap. "Yo, yo, my name's Elite. I've got sick rhymes, don't need to cheat. I power up my rifle with a gigawatt, I take one shot and the Squids all drop. BOOM!"

"OK, OK, Stormzy!" Brain said. He was always irritated by Elite's exuberance.

"Like you know anything about rapping, brainiac."

"Poetry is closely related to mathematics," Brain said, polishing his glasses on a lens cloth. "For instance, iambic pentameter has ten syllables per line."

"*Boring!*" Elite groaned.

"Maybe if you could count to ten, you'd understand it."

Casey could see how rattled and nervous her teammates were. She knew they needed to work together to have any hope of winning. Cheeze must have been thinking the same thing because he turned on his headset and got their attention with a battle cry.

"Who are we?" he asked into his mic. "I said, WHO ARE WE?"

"THE GHOST REAPERS!" they all shouted in unison, except Pete, who was a moment behind the rest of them, his voice like a faint echo. He sounded scared and overwhelmed. Casey could see he was totally out of his depth up there in the spotlight. She pushed her way to the front of the crowd, trying to get his attention.

"Pete, wait, you don't have to do this…" she shouted. But she was drowned out by a klaxon followed by a familiar robotic voice: a voice everyone knew from the game.

"Preparing drop pod launch. On my mark: Five … four … three … two … one … DROP!"

And with that the game began.

* * *

44

In *SkyWake*, everyone had a dedicated role to play: assault, shield tank, sniper, medic, hacker. The key was to work together.

The game's backstory was simple. On a distant planet called Hosin, two alien races were fighting an endless war. On one side were the Arcturians, better known as the Red Eyes. They were humanoid soldiers in bulky black armour. On the other side were the Bactu, tentacled monsters with telepathic powers. They were nicknamed Squids.

The two races had been locked in a deadly war for years. Now the Red Eyes' army was closing in on Hosin, the Squids' homeworld, in a final attempt to wipe them out for good.

What made *SkyWake* so thrilling wasn't its story; it was how real it felt. The weapons, the environments and the action were incredibly immersive. You didn't need to play it for long before you felt ready to go to Hosin and join the fight yourself.

Casey watched the match as it unfolded on the TV screens. The Ghost Reapers, playing as the Red Eyes, were launching from an orbiting spaceship onto the planet below. Their drop pods streaked through the atmosphere, their undersides charring black as they plummeted towards an alien beach of purple sand.

Strike Force, playing as the Squids, were already on the beach preparing their defences.

To win the battle, the Red Eyes would have to break through the Squids' defences and storm their control centre at the top of the beachhead. If they captured it, they'd be victorious. To get there, though, they had to fight through fortified bunkers, dodge artillery fire and avoid being eliminated by the enemy team.

Two alien suns, a vast pink one and a smaller red one, hung in the sky as the team's drop pods thudded onto the beach. The metal canisters cracked open into segments and the Red Eye soldiers, controlled by the Ghost Reapers, stepped out into the Squids' artillery fire.

Pete led his teammates along the beach, shouting orders over his headset. As team leader, it was his job to co-ordinate the attack.

"Fish, put your shield up. Elite, take out the sentry turrets. Cheeze, set up some radars."

Fish's energy shield popped out of the baton in his hand and stretched out in front of them in an enormous, protective rectangle of blue light. Elite's sniper rifle cracked as he destroyed the sentry turrets positioned in the sand dunes. Cheeze tossed out a couple of portable radars, giving them a good view of the map's hidden dangers.

The beach map was designed to provide the attackers with several different routes to the control centre. That gave you a chance to confuse the enemy. But if you hung around in one spot too long, the Squids would hit you hard with their artillery fire. The trick was to keep moving.

Casey hoped Pete knew that.

As the Ghost Reapers advanced along the sand, explosions erupted all around them. Strike Force was shelling them from the cliffs at the top of the beach. Cheeze and Elite took damage. Their screens were flashing red.

"This way," Pete called into his mic as he led them into cover behind a defensive bunker, half buried in the purple sand. "Let's regroup and reload. Brain, heal everyone up."

"We need to advance," Fish said. "Get behind my shield."

"No!" shouted Pete. "I want everyone healed first."

"We're going to die if we don't move," Brain said. "Statistically, our chances of surviving while standing in one place are—"

"It's OK," Pete told them. "They don't know where we are. Trust me."

KABOOM! An enormous green plasma explosion ripped around them. Strike Force's artillery guns had zeroed in on them. Pete jumped out of his seat in surprise. The headset, too big for his head, dropped to the floor.

Then, in the blink of an eye, everything fell apart.

"Enemies ahead," Brain warned.

"Taking fire from the flank!" yelled Elite.

"We need a plan!" Cheeze shouted, hammering his controls as he tried to return fire.

"Shield taking damage," Fish cried as his energy barrier crackled. "It won't last for ever."

On the stage, the Ghost Reapers looked up from their screens at Pete. He was struggling to get his headset back on.

"Yo, Casey," Elite called. "We need orders."

Pete stared at his screen. The explosions in the game reflected over his terrified face. He froze.

"Casey!"

"Give me a second, give me a second," Pete muttered under his breath. His eyes flitted over the map in the corner of his screen. He didn't have time to think. Everyone was jabbering in his ears. The artillery shells were exploding around him.

"Go in the bunker," Pete ordered.

"No!" Casey shouted from the crowd of spectators. But no one was listening.

5

WILL THE REAL CASEY_FLOW PLEASE STAND UP?

Casey had been playing video games long enough to know what a choke point was. Designers built them into maps, funnelling players from opposing teams into areas where they'd be forced to duke it out. They could be hallways or tunnels or bridges, anywhere with plenty of different angles to defend and attack.

Casey knew that the bunker into which Pete was sending the team was a massive choke point. It led to a maze of tunnels running under the beach and it was the perfect place for the Squids to gain the upper hand. Using their telepathic abilities, the Squids could wreak serious havoc on the Red Eye team. A blast of Mind Control would make you attack your own squad, while Confusion would temporarily invert your controls, making everything work the opposite way round. You could only navigate the tunnels successfully by splitting the Red Eye team in two. One group went into the underground maze while the other group stayed on the beach to distract the enemy. That way, you could sneak up on the Squids before they knew you were coming. What you never did was storm into the tunnel in a big group. Not unless you wanted to die.

"Open the bunker door!" Pete shouted to his teammates. Cheeze, the hacker, ran to the computerized lock. It would take a few seconds for his electronic toolkit to unlock the mechanism.

"I'm pinned down!" Brain hollered as he was blasted by incoming fire.

"Elite!" Pete yelled. "We need you."

"On it," Elite whispered into his mic. His eyes narrowed as he leaned towards his screen. "This is gonna be play of the game."

Casey watched on a huge monitor as Elite's sniper crawled through the sand on his belly. He raised his alien sniper rifle and stared down its computerized sights as he targeted a Squid slithering towards him.

PSSSSHHHHTTTT!

The alien hit the deck, tentacles flailing. Casey jumped out of her seat and cheered. The rest of the crowd did too. It was an incredible shot.

On the stage, one of Xander's teammates shouted in fury and ripped off his headset. There were no respawns in this match. He was out of action for the rest of the game.

"They call me the silent killa," Elite rapped into his headset, *"cos I'm all thrilla, don't pack no filla..."*

"Stop showboating," Brain ordered. "Not helpful."

"Hey, brainiac, a little respect. I just saved your butt."

"Hurry up with the bunker," Pete pleaded.

Casey, watching from the crowd, tugged on her hoodie sleeves as the hack continued.

"We're in," Cheeze said as the fortified steel entrance slid open. "Throwing a tarantula."

He tossed something that looked like a grenade towards a Squid that was camping in the shadows in the bunker. As it landed, the grenade sprouted spindly metal legs and transformed into a tarantula-like robot, scuttling across the bunker, too quick for the Squid. When the spider bot was close enough, it pounced, paralysing the tentacled alien with a poisoned bite.

Another of Xander's teammates pushed away his keyboard in frustration as the Squid hit the floor.

"Two down, three to go," Brain murmured calmly.

Maybe they don't need you after all, Casey thought to herself.

"Inside!" Pete shouted to the team. He was beginning to get into the swing of giving orders, and was enjoying the fact that everyone was listening to him. He covered the team with his plasma rifle as they dived into the bunker one by one. Then he turned and followed them himself.

"No, don't take the whole squad in there!" Casey warned. But it was no use. Pete couldn't hear her over the noise of the arena.

Casey felt her stomach lurch. Without anyone outside on the beach to create a distraction, the Squids would slither underground after the Ghost Reapers and the tunnels would become a choke point.

She looked up at the giant screen and saw Xander's face filling it. The gamer legend licked his lips like a python preparing to swallow an unsuspecting goat. Xander knew he had the Ghost Reapers exactly where he wanted them. Even with only three players, his team would be able to overwhelm them underground.

Pete led the team further into the tunnels. He had no idea he was doing anything wrong. At the skill rank he usually played in, you could get away with this kind of strategy. At this level, though, the enemy team would never fall for it.

By the time the other Ghost Reapers realized Pete's mistake, it was too late.

"Hold on," Brain said, looking around the bunker on his monitor. "Why are we all here? Who's attacking the beach?"

There was a collective groan from the others as it dawned on them what had happened.

"Casey!" Fish shouted at Pete. "You total muppet head!"

"What's the problem?" Pete asked. "We'll push on up the tunnel and take them out."

Nobody moved. This was a rookie mistake. The kind of mistake Casey Flow would never make. Confusion and fear swept over the Ghost Reapers.

And that was the moment Xander's team attacked.

The thing Pete hated most about Squids was the sound they made as they moved. They propelled themselves through the tunnels like angry octopuses, their tentacles producing a sucking kind of slurp as they made contact with the floors and walls. It was the stuff of nightmares.

The sound filled Pete's headset as Xander and

his two surviving Squid comrades slithered out of the gloom. Xander grabbed Cheeze first, wrapping a tentacle around him and lifting the Red Eye soldier off his feet, choking him until he was out of the match. At his monitor, Cheeze yelled as his avatar died and the kill cam popped up.

"I've got this," Elite said cockily, running forward to no-scope them with his sniper rifle.

"Stay behind my shield," Fish warned. But it was too late. Elite's shots went wide and the two Squids blasted him. He was out too.

Pete saw his downed comrades and panicked. Brain and Fish bravely tried to hold the Squids back, but Xander's special ultimate ability was now fully charged. He hit a button on his keyboard and used the Squids' Mind Control powers to take control of Brain's Red Eye soldier. Brain's screen turned white around the edges and throbbed like a migraine as his avatar fell under Xander's power. His controls went dead.

"They've zombied me!" Brain cried, looking on powerlessly as his Red Eye soldier lifted his energy sword and stabbed Fish in the back.

"Hey! Friendly fire!" Fish shouted, incensed. He spun around with his shield up to defend himself, but that left his rear unprotected. The Squids blasted him from behind.

"Fall back," Pete yelled, ducking in his seat as a barrage of Squid fire flew past him in the game. He was so panicked that he was actually shaking. "Retreat!" he shouted again, but no one was listening. Brain and Fish ignored him, fighting just to stay alive. Nobody was working as a team any more. It was utter chaos.

Casey, watching from the audience, realized her brother had done the worst thing a leader could do. He'd lost control of his squad. She pushed further through the crowd, elbowing people out of her way.

It was time for the real Casey Flow to stand up.

She jumped onto the stage, ignoring the shouts from Lee and the eSports officials and yanking the headset off Pete.

"This is Casey Flow," she told her team, talking into the mic as she pushed her brother out of his seat.

"The *real* Casey Flow. We only have one shot to win this. Just do what I say."

From behind their bank of computers, the Ghost Reapers stared at her in surprise.

"What's going on?" Fish demanded.

"Later," Casey said firmly. "Right now, we've got

a match to win. Brain, you're my decoy."

She glanced over at Brain. The white tinge around the edge of his screen was disappearing and his game screen was returning to normal. Xander was losing his psychic control over Brain's avatar.

"What are you on about?" he asked, his eyes widening behind his lenses.

"Just get a psi grenade ready," she told him.

Casey, now controlling Pete's Red Eye soldier, dived into cover and blasted at the Squids with her plasma rifle. Unlike Pete, she was a great shot. The enemy aliens slithered away, surprised. Casey hammered the bunker's keypad lock so her team could retreat back outside.

"What are you *doing*?" Fish shouted.

"We're going to mind-melt them," Casey said.

"What do you know about mind-melting?" Brain asked in surprise.

"Just do what I say!" Casey yelled in a tone that shut them all up.

His shield up, Fish moved sideways to protect her. Brain fell in behind him. The Squids' fire was absorbed by the shield. Behind them, the keypad bleeped and the heavy steel outer doors opened up. Sunlight from the beach streamed into the bunker.

"On me!" Casey ordered. "Pull back to the crater."

She slammed through the doors, vanishing into the sand.

Fish slowly followed her, walking backwards, his shield still up. It crackled as the Squids concentrated their fire on him. Brain stared along the beach and saw a crater in the sand where an artillery shell had exploded. It would be deep enough to hide them, but not for long.

Back in the bunker, the Squids slithered towards the door, still firing. Xander's team moved confidently, convinced they had them trapped.

"My shield's almost down," Fish called as he reached the rim of the crater, his combat boots sending an avalanche of purple sand tumbling into it. Brain, next to him, pulled a psi grenade off his belt and searched for Casey in the crater. But it was empty.

"Casey? Where are you?" he shouted into his headset.

"On the roof."

Fish and Brain looked up and saw Casey's avatar standing on top of the bunker, high above the Squids. The enemy team hadn't seen her. If any of them used their telepathic abilities, though, she'd be toast.

"I've got the grenade ready," Brain whispered, excited by Casey's daring.

"We've got a choice," Casey told the boys. "I can try and take them all out from up here…"

"That's a big risk," Brain said. "Odds must be a hundred to one, at least."

"… or we can decoy," Casey continued. "But that'll mean you both die."

On the stage, in real life, Fish and Brain exchanged a glance.

"Decoy," they confirmed in unison.

"You're sure?"

"Do it," Brain said firmly. "No way you can take them all, even with the height advantage."

"Just don't mess it up," Fish warned.

"Trust me," Casey said. "I've got this."

As the Squids slithered towards the bunker, Brain threw his psi grenade.

"Fire in the hole!" he yelled as he hit his keyboard.

Before the grenade even touched the ground, Casey had jumped off the far side of the bunker roof. She hit the sprint button and thundered along the beach, dodging fire from the automated sentry turrets that lined her path.

Back at the crater, the psi grenade exploded in a flash of green light. It would scramble the Squids' telepathic powers for a good thirty seconds. Without their special abilities, they wouldn't know where Casey was on the map.

It wasn't long. But it was all the edge she needed.

"They got me!" Brain cried. Casey glanced over at his screen. Xander had slithered into the crater and wrapped a tentacle around him. Even without their psi powers, the Squids were deadly.

Fish was still fighting but he was almost out of power. "Shield down!" he shouted in panic as it went offline. He was dead in seconds.

It was all on Casey now.

She sprinted along the beach towards the control room. Behind her, the Squids slithered left and right, searching the sand for her. She could hear Xander on the other side of the stage shouting at his teammates angrily. He realized they'd been had.

"I'm almost there," Casey whispered into her headset as she leaned in towards her monitor. "Almost, almost, almost…"

She was operating on pure instinct. Pete clung on to the back of her chair, willing her on. The rest of the team, all out of the match now, watched her progress on their own screens, rapt.

Casey's Red Eye soldier ran up the stairs to the control room and pulled out a standard-issue hacking tool. As an assault player, her hacking skill was low, which meant it would take a few seconds longer than if Cheeze had been doing it. While she was crouched at the doors, she'd be vulnerable. She watched as her hacking tool shot out an infrared beam and started to unscramble the door lock.

Behind her, a Squid slithered into view. Xander had guessed her plan.

"Move!" shouted Pete.

"Get out of there!" hollered Elite.

Xander reached a tentacle towards Casey's crouched avatar. His psi powers were still out of action after Brain's grenade, but that wouldn't stop him from launching a melee attack on her with his tentacles.

Casey looked from Xander to the hack.

It was at 96 per cent.

If she broke off now, she'd have to restart from scratch. Could she make it?

The tentacle slithered along the ground towards her. Casey felt her body, her real body in real life, tense up. The tentacle got closer and closer and …

Bleep! The control room doors unlocked. Casey swapped the hacking tool for her Red Eye energy sword. The game's animation took half a second to complete and then the weapon was in her hands.

The energy sword fired up in a plume of curved blue light.

FWWWWWOM! She slashed the tentacle just as it wrapped around her leg. It fell to the floor, seared off the Squid's body in a flash of heat.

"You did it!" shouted Brain.

"Ya belter!" Fish yelled.

Xander, behind his monitor, screamed in fury.

Casey's soldier dived into the control room and the doors slid shut behind her. **VICTORY!** flashed up on her screen.

"We did it!" she screamed, jumping out of her seat and punching the air. The Ghost Reapers did the same, hugging one another as if they'd just scored the winning goal in the Champions League final.

The rest of the tournament zone erupted. They'd just seen the most dramatic *SkyWake* match of the day.

As the applause echoed around the arena, Casey pulled off her headset. Her body was shaking, pumped full of adrenaline. She felt ready to take on the whole world. She looked around at her team in excitement, preparing to run over and hug them all.

But the boys were all staring at her in shock.

"You've got a lot of explaining to do, Casey Flow,"

Brain said. And for the first time that day he was talking to her, not Pete.

6

CHEATS NEVER PROSPER

"You used a voice changer?" Brain said angrily as the team regrouped on the edge of the tournament zone.

"I can't believe you lied to us," Fish chipped in. "We've been playing together for over six months."

"It just ain't right," agreed Elite. "I thought we were fam."

Casey saw their anger and realized that saving the match had come at a big cost.

"I'm sorry," she whispered, unable to meet their gaze. "I thought it would help me fit in. I never dreamed we'd meet in real life…"

"So you're saying you would have kept on pretending if we hadn't busted you?" Fish spat out the words, his face flushing a deep shade of crimson.

"Yes," said Casey. "I mean, no… Well, maybe."

She felt like she was drowning. A trickle of sweat

ran down her back. She saw Cheeze looking up at her.

"Did you really think we'd stop playing with you if we found out you were a girl?" he asked, in a disappointed voice. "I wouldn't have cared…" He looked at the others. Elite and Brain shrugged and nodded in agreement.

"Well, I would have done," Fish said, crossing his arms over his chest.

"Why?" Brain asked in surprise. "Because she's a girl?"

"Because she's a liar. I hate liars."

"But you don't like girls much either, do you?" Cheeze said.

Fish reddened even more. "She could have told us the truth when she met us today," he complained, unable to let it go. "But she kept on lying. She even got her little brother to lie for her."

Casey looked down at Pete. He was standing on the edge of the group, biting his lip like he might cry.

Xander strutted over, interrupting them.

"GG, good game, you guys. Shame the only way you could beat me was by cheating," he added cockily. He was shadowed by one his teammates, a lanky teenager holding a video camera. It was one of those fancy 4K models that pro YouTubers use.

"We didn't cheat," Cheeze snapped, eager to defend the team's honour.

"OMG. So, like, changing a player in the middle of a match isn't cheating?" Xander mugged to the camera, pulling a shocked face. "Who knew?"

"It was just a mistake in our team line-up," Brain explained, although he clearly didn't think it was a very convincing argument.

"Hey, bruv, get out of my face," Elite said as the video kid moved in for a close-up.

"He's just shooting footage for my stream," Xander explained breezily. "You know, I thought today was gonna be real boring. But you morons have done me a favour. My subscriber numbers will go way up when people see how I was cheated out of a legit win."

"Our pleasure," Cheeze said, sarcastically.

"So you're the real Casey Flow?" Xander asked Casey, pushing his fringe out of his eyes. He extended a hand. "I'm Xander Kane."

"I know. I've seen you on YouTube."

"You and a million other people."

"One million, two hundred and seventy-four," corrected the video kid, checking his phone. "Accordinging to the live view count."

Casey didn't like Xander much, but she shook

the hand he offered her. Her dad had taught her that a firm handshake was a sign you could be trusted. Xander's grip was as limp as a dead fish.

"Those were some pretty amazing moves back there," he said. "How did you do it?"

"I don't really know," Casey said. "Sometimes, when I'm playing, it's like something takes over and I stop thinking about what I'm doing. It just sort of … *happens*. My dad used to call it the 'flow'. That feeling you get when you're totally at one with the game."

She realized they didn't have a clue what she was talking about. She fell silent, feeling like an idiot.

"So what happens now?" Brain asked, breaking the awkward silence.

"That's for them to decide," Xander said, nodding towards Lee and the eSports officials, who were huddled together on the stage. "But if you ask me, you should get ready to go home. Try not to take it personally." He crossed his fingers together into another X-sign and headed off to rejoin his clan.

As the YouTuber walked away, Cheeze flicked an angry V-sign behind his back in response.

"I've always hated that guy," he muttered to nobody in particular.

* * *

Lee and the eSports officials took for ever to confer. They bent their heads together as they discussed the situation. After a few minutes, Lee glanced over at the Ghost Reapers. He stared hard at Casey. Her heart sank. It didn't look good.

She felt a hand tug on her sleeve. It was Pete. She hadn't spoken to him since the match ended.

"Casey?"

"Not now," she said.

"I was only trying to help…"

"By pretending to be me?"

"You told me not to give you away," he replied, hurt.

He was right; she had.

"Just leave me alone," Casey said sharply. A replay of her victory looped over and over on the giant monitor. She stared at it, numb. Her amazing win now felt like a crushing loss. Deep in thought, she didn't see Pete pushing his way into the crowd.

Ten minutes later, the officials reached a decision. A burst of static crackled around the tournament zone, silencing the audience. Lee stepped back onstage, microphone in hand, his suit shimmering under the bright lights.

"What a round!" he exclaimed. "Drama. Suspense.

Unexpected twists and turns. We were on the edge of our seats." He paused a moment and cleared his throat. "Now, as you all saw, the last match was a little unusual. But the judges have conferred and, after consulting the tournament rules, they have reached a final decision..."

He paused theatrically. The crowd held its breath. Casey shut her eyes. She couldn't bear the anticipation any longer.

"It is with regret that I have to announce that the Ghost Reapers have been disqualified."

The tournament zone erupted into chaos. There were boos and shouts from the audience who were clearly now keen for the Ghost Reapers to win. Xander and the rest of Strike Force didn't care. They leaped into the air, hugging one another in celebration.

Casey opened her eyes again. It felt as if the room was swimming around her. The boys stared at one another in shock. Despite their dramatic win, they were being thrown out! Their dream was crumbling in front of them.

"Better luck next time, guys," Lee said as he hopped off the stage.

"What? You mean that's it?" Elite asked, looking like he could cry. "It's over, just like that?"

"We've got complimentary merch bags waiting for you outside," Lee told them.

"There must be someone we can appeal to," Brain said, glancing around. "Perhaps if we explain the situation..."

Fish shouldered his way through his teammates to get to Casey. His face shone bright red with anger. "This is your fault," he said, jabbing a finger in her face. "You and your little brother stuffed it up for all of us."

"Leave him out of this," Casey said, springing to Pete's defence. She turned around to reassure her brother. Maybe she could still make this right with him.

It was then that Casey realized Pete had vanished.

7

NEVER BRING A SANDWICH
TO A GUNFIGHT

As Pete ran through the tournament zone, hot, angry tears filled his eyes. He barged through the gamers, wriggling into the crowd until he couldn't see Casey any more. He hadn't meant to ruin everything for his sister – he'd only been trying to help. But she blamed him, just like she always did. He was fed up of her pushing him around. *Casey Flow,* the big sister. *Casey Flow,* the great gamer. *Casey Flow,* the favourite daughter. She thought she was so cool with her bubblegum-blue streaks. Well, she'd lose her cool when she realized he'd gone.

He hurried towards a fire exit and shoved it open, not even stopping to think if it was alarmed. No bells rang out. The doors swung shut behind him.

The exit led into a windowless corridor. He jogged along it for a minute or two, turning corners at random. Finally, out of breath, he stopped and leaned against the wall next to a noticeboard covered in staff rotas. He guessed he must be in a service area that ran behind the shops.

Casey would never find him now. He imagined how badly Mum would freak out when she heard that Casey had lost him. She'd go nuts.

It was very still and silent in the service corridor, especially after the hustle and bustle of the tournament zone. As Pete walked on, looking for a door that would take him back to the shops, he began to feel on edge. There was something eerie about the empty corridors and their cold, breeze-block walls. He wondered what would happen if he bumped into a security guard. He sped up, keen not to find out.

The next corridor was even gloomier. The electric strip light on the ceiling was on the blink. It hummed and buzzed like an angry insect, flickering on and off and casting everything in intermittent shadows as if there was some nearby interference.

He shivered, feeling cold and slightly anxious.

"Are you with the tournament?" demanded a gruff voice.

Pete froze. He was about to apologize and make up a story about being lost when he realized that the voice wasn't talking to him. It was coming from around the next corner. He crept forwards and peered around the wall … and stopped in his tracks.

A security guard stood in the middle of the corridor, facing off a group of five cosplayers in Red Eye outfits. The guard held a chunky marinara meatball sub. The Red Eyes held chunky plasma rifles.

"This is a restricted area," the guard said, hiding the sandwich behind his back and wiping his mouth guiltily. "You need to go back the way you came."

The cosplayers stared at him, their red eyes burning. They were at least two metres tall and towered over him.

The guard cleared his throat. "Come on now, lads. I know you're supposed to be 'aliens-from-another-planet' but there's no need to be silly about this. Rules are rules, whatever galaxy you're from."

No one moved.

The guard's face formed into a scowl. He was out of patience. "I'm giving you five seconds to head back the way you came," he said firmly. In the silence that followed, Pete counted to five in his head. Still none of them had moved.

"Fine," the guard said, reaching for the radio on his belt with his free hand. "You've only got yourselves to blame." He spoke into the radio. "Control. I need back-up. Got a couple of trespassers here."

As he finished speaking, the radio released a burst of high-pitched static. Surprised, the Red Eyes raised their plasma rifles in a rattle of hardware. The guard stepped backwards. His Adam's apple bobbed in his throat.

"What do you think you're doing?" he asked, his voice cracking with fear.

"Fecht ictu," hissed one of the Red Eyes in a mechanical tone that was strange and guttural, like Welsh mixed with Mongolian.

"It's just a radio," the guard said, lifting it slowly into the air in an attempt to prove it wasn't a weapon. His other hand still held the foot-long sub sandwich. That went into the air too. A stray meatball fell out and splatted on the floor in a pool of blood-red marinara sauce.

For a moment, Pete wondered if this was all just a joke. It was the sort of prank Xander might put on his channel to entertain his subscribers. Yet something about it didn't seem right.

"Let's talk about this…" The guard was trying to stay calm but was visibly shaking. Pete moved slightly, trying to get a better view of the cosplayers. As he did, the guard spotted him. The man's eyes darted sideways, telling Pete to get away.

Just then, the guard's radio squawked back into life.

"Mick?" said a woman's voice crossly. "I can't see you on my monitors. Where are you? You'd better not be snacking in the corridors again…"

The Red Eyes' grip on their weapons tightened.

"Run!" the guard shouted to Pete.

At the same moment, there was a *whoosh* that sucked all the air out of the corridor. Green plasma fire burst from a Red Eye rifle.

Pete didn't wait to see what happened next. He raced back the way he'd come, his brain feeling like it was about to explode with the insanity of it all.

These guys weren't Red Eye cosplayers … they were *real* Red Eyes!

As he put his head down and tore towards the next junction, he heard that same *whoosh* as another plasma blast flew after him. He felt its searing heat on the back of his neck and threw himself to the ground.

The plasma fire sailed over his head and smashed into the breeze blocks, melting right through them. Pete glimpsed a guy on the other side of the wall, standing in the changing rooms of a clothing store trying on trousers. He stood with one leg in and one leg out of a pair of skinny jeans. The shocked "O" of his mouth matched the hole in the breeze blocks.

Pete scrabbled to his feet and ran blindly on, desperate to get back to the tournament zone. He had to warn the others. He reached the next corner, glancing over his shoulder to see if he was being followed.

"Oompf!" he grunted as he crashed into another Red Eye coming around the bend. The impact knocked Pete off his feet. It was like colliding with Mount Everest. He looked up and saw an overseer, a Red Eye commander. Over his armoured suit, the alien wore a long black cloak with a hood that came up over his head, totally obscuring his face. The inside of the hood was shrouded in impenetrable darkness. All you could see in it were three red dots arranged to form a triangle.

"Sorry," Pete said automatically. His brain was still living in a sane world where you apologized when you bumped into someone.

The overseer said nothing. He just stared down at Pete, the triangular dots glowing as a lattice of red lasers shot out. They dazzled Pete, forcing him to close his eyes. He kept them shut as the lasers moved down his chest. There was a bleep as they read the QR code on Casey's **COMPETITOR** ID badge.

Pete felt something cold and heavy snap around his neck. He opened his eyes and stifled a terrified yelp as he saw a black metal loop around his throat. It was shaped like a D-lock, one of those curved metal bars that cyclists use to stop their bikes being stolen. An orange LED flashed on its side. Pete tugged at it helplessly, panic rising in his chest.

He was a prisoner.

Behind him, on the other side of the hole that had been blasted in the wall, a shop assistant appeared. She stood beside the man in the changing room and stared at the overseer in disbelief. Then she quickly pulled out her handset and dialled three digits in quick succession.

"Get me the police," she said.

The overseer glared at his unwelcome audience and grunted with displeasure. Then he touched a finger to the side of his hood and gave a command in his harsh alien language. Pete wasn't sure what the word meant. But something told him it wasn't good news.

8

CONFIRMED INCURSION

As soon as they realized Pete was missing, the Ghost Reapers stopped bickering and helped Casey search the tournament zone.

But there was no sign of him anywhere.

Casey swore under her breath, convinced he'd done it just to get back at her. Her mum was going to kill her for letting him run away.

"Let's check the shops," Brain suggested, leading the group out onto the first-floor balcony. Casey gazed over the railings into the atrium in the centre of the building. The empty space stretched from the ground floor all the way up to the glass ceiling. She could see each of the other seven floors above her. They were teeming with crowds of shoppers.

Pete could be anywhere.

Cheeze rolled up beside her. "Does he have a phone?"

"Mum won't let him have one until he goes to senior school."

"He'll be here somewhere," he reassured her. "We'll find him, I promise."

Casey watched the crowds below as they entered and exited through the main doors. So many people... Her heart hammered against her ribs.

"Could he have left the building?" Cheeze asked, following her gaze. "Maybe he went to the bus stop or a Tube station."

"I don't know," Casey said despairingly. "I've managed to get everything wrong today."

Cheeze reached out to pat her arm shyly.

As he did, there was a thundering crash above them. They looked up to see the glass ceiling smash open. Shards of glass plummeted into the atrium below like a crystal waterfall. There were screams as shoppers ran for cover.

Casey and Cheeze stared in shock as a swarm of shiny metal drones flew through the jagged glass. They darted left and right, fanning out in packs and whizzing through the shopping centre at speed.

"Watch out!" yelled Cheeze as a drone flew towards Casey's head. It was sleek and metallic and the size of a junior rugby ball. It whizzed past her ear, centimetres from hitting her. Then it raced across the balcony through the startled, screaming crowds, dipping wildly as it tried to avoid two men coming out of Currys carrying a boxed-up sixty-inch TV. It dipped so low under the cardboard box that its belly scraped along the marble floor. Weaving this way and that through shoppers' ankles, it attempted to regain its balance before it was blindsided by a dad pushing a pram.

Knocked off course, the drone spun sideways and ended up in the nearby food court. It tumbled across a table where a family was eating, spilling the kids' Happy Meals onto the floor.

"What the hell *are* they?" Fish shouted, ducking behind the balcony rail beside Brain and Elite as more of the drones flew in through the roof.

Casey ran to the food court to get a better look. Cheeze followed, pumping hard on his wheelchair's tyres to keep up. Casey pushed through the family of diners gathering around the machine.

The drone lay on the floor, flapping about like a wounded insect. It was smeared in ketchup and splodges of strawberry milkshake. A thin curl of black smoke escaped from its insides.

The drone had a sleek metal body and a large circular lens at its front that reminded Casey of a giant

Cyclops's eye. On its chassis two LEDs blinked once, twice, and then went out.

"Is it dead?" Casey wondered aloud. She gingerly slid the toe of her trainer under its battered body and flipped it over. Nothing happened. Then, with a bleep, the drone sputtered back into life. It launched and began to hover a few centimetres above the ground, wobbling.

"Careful, it could be dangerous," Cheeze said as the family moved in for a closer look. He opened one of the side pockets on his wheelchair and pulled out a screwdriver, brandishing it like a weapon. "Stay back!" he warned the machine.

The drone retreated a bit and stared at the crowd for a moment as it bobbed in mid-air. It emitted a series of shrill electronic beeps and whistles. It sounded like it was laughing at them.

Then, with a sudden *whoosh*, it spun around and charged back towards the balcony where the other boys were still crouched. It sailed over their heads and then dropped over the side of the railings like a falling stone.

Casey ran to the edge just in time to see it joining the rest of the drones as they whizzed across the ground floor. They moved as one, like a swarm of angry bees. Panicked shoppers ducked and ran to get out of their way. Some even jumped into the indoor fountain as the drones flew over their heads.

"They're heading for the main doors!" she called, running to the escalators. "Let's follow them!"

"Wait!" Cheeze shouted, spinning his wheelchair around. "I don't do escalators."

But Casey, caught up in the thrill of the chase, wasn't listening.

The drones smashed through the main doors into the car park. Once outside, they flew up into the sky, momentarily blocking out the sun. Casey arrived to see them hovering in mid-air, as if waiting for something.

Sirens rang out in the distance. Police or paramedics or fire engines, or perhaps all three, were clearly on their way to the shopping centre. Casey looked over at the TV news vans. Reporters were staring and pointing at the drones, shouting at their camera operators to get filming.

At the same moment, the doors of the black minivan Casey had seen earlier burst open and the buzz-cut military man jumped out. He surveyed the scene with a steely gaze, apparently unfazed.

The drones spread out to form a large circle, stretching all the way around the building. They hovered in evenly spaced formation above the car park for a moment. Then, without warning, they fell to the ground, one by one. It was as if they'd all simultaneously lost power. Some hit the tarmac in the car park. Others fell onto the paved pedestrian areas. People screamed and ran for cover.

Through the panicked crowd, Casey saw the buzz-cut man again. He was the only person not running away in fright. He noticed her staring at him and saw the questioning look on her face.

"Come with me," he ordered her, stretching out his hand as the drones rained down around them. "Quickly!"

"What's going on?" Casey demanded, ignoring his hand. Everything was happening too fast. The last drone fell right between them. They both stared at it. Casey recognized its ketchup-splattered chassis. It was the one she'd seen upstairs. It burrowed into the tarmac with a crunch and a hiss as metal prongs protruded from its body and tethered it securely to the ground like a limpet on a rock.

"There's no time," the man said, his voice urgent.

Casey hesitated, glancing over her shoulder at the shopping centre. Frightened shoppers were dashing in all directions trying to find safety. It was total chaos.

"My brother's still inside," she said.

"You have to hurry," said the man, insistently. His outstretched hand hung in the air. All the drones had embedded themselves in the tarmac. They lay there waiting for something.

"No," Casey said, shaking her head. "I can't leave Pete..."

The drone at her feet made a humming sound. Its body rippled with a strange blue energy. All around the car park, the other drones were doing the same thing. Then a beam of blue light shot out of each drone, linking together to form an enormous dome that stretched high over the shopping centre.

Casey fell back in surprise as the wall of energy cut her off from the buzz-cut man. She realized instantly what it was.

A force field.

It was like someone had put a goldfish bowl over the building, dividing the car park in half and separating the mall from the rest of the city. She realized she was trapped inside it. Several shoppers around her screamed, separated from their friends and family on the other side of the energy wall.

Casey reached a finger out towards the force field and felt her skin tingle and burn before it even made contact. She jerked her hand back, scared.

From the other side, the buzz-cut man shook his head at her. He started to speak but his voice was drowned out by the sound of four police vehicles screeching into the car park, sirens blaring. There was a squeal of tyres as the driver of the lead car saw the force field blocking her way. She yanked the steering wheel hard and hit the brakes, putting the car into a tailspin. As the vehicle's rear end skidded into the force field, its back tyres exploded and the metal frame around the boot melted away. Droplets of molten metal hit the ground and ran into the grooves and cracks in the tarmac.

The other three police cars peeled off left and right, narrowly avoiding a crash. Casey was extremely glad she hadn't touched the energy field with her bare hand.

Quick as a flash, the buzz-cut man jumped into action and ran towards the wrecked police car. He pulled the police officers out of the vehicle, moving with the confidence of someone who'd been in dangerous situations before. He helped them to safety behind the cover of a TV news van, a split second before their ruined police car exploded. Chunks of burning metal rained over the car park.

Casey ducked instinctively, although she didn't need to. None of the wreckage could penetrate the dome above her. It simply disintegrated as it hit the force field. She looked up into the sky, following the curve of the dome as it stretched above West Point's roof.

As she did, she saw the same shimmer that she'd noticed earlier. There was no mistaking it this time. The air glitched and rippled as an enormous spaceship decloaked on the roof of the building. It was as if it had been hidden there all along. It sat under the tip of the dome, happy to reveal itself now that it was safe beneath the energy field's protective umbrella.

Casey blinked in astonishment. Shoppers on both sides of the dome looked up and gasped. One man even pulled out his phone and started to take pictures with it. The spaceship was wider than the shopping centre and its wingspan stretched over the edges of the roof. At one end it had a long, pointed nose that made it look like a giant bird of prey.

Casey recognized it immediately. She'd seen it more times than she could count. It was an Arcturian dropship, straight out of *SkyWake*.

But that wasn't possible!

How could something from a video game be here,

in real life, in the middle of London? On the other side of the force field, over by the TV news vans, she saw the buzz-cut man. He was staring up at the roof too, as he'd done earlier that morning.

"Just a trick of the light?" Casey shouted at him angrily. Something told her that he'd known about the dropship's presence all along.

"You should have come with me," he said, his voice slightly distorted as it came through the force field. He shook his head at her in annoyance then turned and walked away. As he did, he pulled out his phone.

"This is Dreyfus," he said to whoever was on the other end of the call. "We have a confirmed incursion."

"Wait!" Casey shouted, but he kept on walking. Just then, a scream rang out from inside the shopping centre. It was followed by a sound that chilled her to the bone. The sound of an Arcturian plasma rifle firing.

"Oh my God. Pete."

9

INSERT COINS TO CONTINUE

The summer before Casey's dad died, he'd taken her to an old video arcade called FunZone. It was hidden down a back street between a barber's shop that looked like it never opened and a fried-chicken joint that looked like it never shut. The arcade was dirty and rundown and a FOR SALE sign hung on the wall outside.

"I used to spend all my pocket money here when I was your age," her dad had whispered as they stood on the pavement outside. "It hasn't changed a bit."

Casey found it hard to imagine her dad ever being her age. He was a tall man with square shoulders, an angular face and playful eyes. It was obvious he was in the army. Not just from the way he moved, precise and full of confidence, but also from the olive-green Royal Engineers T-shirt he wore under his fleece.

"When we get in there, let me do the talking," he instructed as they headed to the entrance. "If we're going to bag this machine at a price that doesn't break the bank, I need to negotiate."

Casey saluted him. "Yessir, Lieutenant, sir."

"*Left*-tenant, not *Loo*-tenant," he corrected her. "You watch too many American movies."

Casey laughed. She was enjoying having her dad to herself. Mum had taken Pete shopping to buy clothes for the new school year. The minute they'd left, her dad had asked Casey if she wanted to go on a "mission". He always called it that when they had adventures together. Before Casey knew what was happening, they had hired a van and driven out here in search of a vintage piece of video-game memorabilia.

The owner of FunZone was a man called Dom. He had long hair and an untidy beard and he smelled like he hadn't had a shower since for ever. As he slurped tea from a chipped mug, he told them how the arcade was closing down and all the machines were being sold off.

"Turns out the land the shop's built on is worth more than the arcade itself," he complained. "Some big-shot developer wants to knock it all down and build 'urban living' apartments here instead. Urban living, my arse."

Casey tried not to giggle. Her dad shot her a stern look, although she could see his eyes twinkling mischievously.

"So what exactly are you looking for, mate?" Dom asked. He waved a grubby hand at the machines lining the walls. "We've got all sorts in here. Racing games, fighting games, shoot 'em ups."

"I don't really know," Casey's dad replied. "I just saw your advert in the paper and I've always fancied owning my own arcade machine. Mind if we have a look around?"

"Help yourself." Dom shrugged. He took another loud slurp from his mug.

Casey knew her dad was playing it cool. He'd explained his tactics as they drove across town. If you looked too eager, the seller would bump up the price. Best to pretend you weren't actually that interested in buying anything. That was why they'd parked the hire van around the corner, out of sight.

Her dad strolled through the arcade, taking his time. He inspected each machine in turn, occasionally smiling to himself as he recognized an old favourite. Most of the titles Casey had never heard of, but she did her best to look interested.

"You in the army?" Dom asked. He was a real talker. It was like he was allergic to silence.

"Royal Engineers."

Casey moved over to an old zombie shooting game called *House of the Dead* and picked up one of its plastic light guns. She wished she had some coins so she could have a quick blast.

"Been out in Iraq? Afghanistan?"

"A little."

"See much action? Shoot anyone?"

"I'm on bomb disposal," her dad explained. "I try to save people, not kill them." He never liked talking about his job.

Dom whistled, impressed. "I wouldn't fancy that. All the money in the world wouldn't be enough to make me risk getting blown up."

Her dad stared sharply at Dom and then glanced at Casey as if to say, *Please don't talk about me getting blown up in front of my daughter.*

Dom shut his mouth, realizing he'd spoken out of turn.

"So, are you a gamer?" he asked, changing the subject. "You don't look like one."

"Soldiers have always had a soft spot for games,"

her dad told him as he checked out a *Street Fighter II* cabinet. "Some of the earliest board games started off as military training tools. Generals used to play chess to teach themselves how to think strategically. It was like a battlefield simulator."

Dom grunted and took another slurp of his tea. "Seen anything you like?"

Casey looked over at her dad. He'd moved into a dark corner of the arcade, near a couple of snooker tables. A dusty cabinet sat in the shadows, long-forgotten. The case was painted blue and red and decorated with flying saucers and giant fuzzy monsters straddling a rocky lunar landscape.

"This," said her dad, patting the machine like it was an old friend. "This is the one I want."

"That piece of junk?" Dom chuckled. "It's virtually prehistoric. I've got loads of better machines in here. That one doesn't even power up any more."

Casey's dad wasn't listening. He placed his hands on the machine's dead controls. They were covered in a thick layer of dust. Casey joined him and took a closer look. Dom was right. It *was* prehistoric.

She inspected the cabinet's casing, searching for a name. It was printed in big yellow letters in a blocky, futuristic font: **SPACE INVADERS**.

*　　*　　*

"I played that game to death when I was younger," Casey's dad had chuckled to himself as they drove the hire van home. The cabinet was strapped in the back. It had taken them half an hour to load it. It weighed a ton.

"I thought we were buying something exciting," Casey complained. "Something like that zombie game I saw. Or even just something that actually works…"

"I'll fix it," he promised. "It just needs some TLC. And it *is* exciting. It's *Space Invaders*. The original arcade classic! You versus a bunch of aliens in a battle to save the world. It doesn't get more exciting than that."

Casey sank back into her seat as the van moved slowly through the weekend traffic. Mum was going to flip out.

When they got back home, the *Space Invaders* machine went straight into the garage. It slotted neatly against the wall in a space between her dad's tool racks. It was as if he'd been planning for its arrival for some time.

"I can't believe you went without me," Pete complained when he saw the cabinet. "How come Casey gets to go looking for arcade games while I'm shopping for school uniform?"

"Because Casey didn't lose her blazer on the bus," his sister reminded him.

"You didn't miss much," their dad said, tousling Pete's hair. "The guy we bought it from smelled of stale kebabs and he never stopped talking. You're here in time for the fun part."

He bent down and unscrewed the cabinet's faceplate, exposing its electrical innards. While he was busy, Pete stuck his tongue out at Casey behind his back.

Seeing him poring over the machine's circuit board with a screwdriver and pliers gave Casey a funny feeling. She imagined this was what he must look like when he was crouched over an improvised explosive device out in Afghanistan.

"Everyone thinks bomb disposal must be tense," he'd told her once. "But the truth is, when I'm doing it, I'm really calm. It's like being in a bubble. You're totally in the zone. You forget about everything else until it's just you and the device. It's only afterwards, when the bomb is defused and it's all over, that you get a bit scared."

Casey knew her dad did an important job, but sometimes she wished he worked in an office like her friends' dads did.

It took their dad twenty minutes to find the problem. "Ah, here it is," he said, looking up at them. "The power supply to the monitor needs to be reattached. Pass me the tools, Pete."

Pete, glad to be helping him, brought the heavy toolbox over. He knelt down beside his dad and peered into the machine.

"Do you want to do something cool?" their dad asked.

"Sure."

"Take that can and spray it inside."

Pete took a spray can from the toolbox. When he squeezed it, a blast of compressed air flew over the circuit board, dislodging decades of dust that swirled around the garage and made him cough.

"Ugh, gross," he complained.

Their dad plugged in a soldering iron and slowly reattached the loose wires onto the circuit board. It was fiddly work.

"OK," he said finally, closing the cabinet back up. "We're ready to go. Who wants to do the honours?"

"Me!" shouted Pete, racing to beat Casey to it.

"Hey, no fair," she complained. "You did the aerosol." She knew she sounded like a kid but it was fun winding her brother up.

Pete didn't listen. He ran over to the power socket and plugged the machine in. When he flicked the switch, the screen lit up and it ran a system check. A few lines of boot-up code scrolled over the monitor as it started up.

"It's only got three colours!" Pete said, unimpressed.

"It doesn't even have that," their dad laughed. "The monitor is black and white. There's a strip of cellophane over the screen to make it look like it's got colours."

The words **INSERT CCOIN** flashed up.

"Hey, they spelled it wrong," Casey said.

"Wait a second," their dad said, his lips twitching into a smile. As they watched, a flying saucer moved across the top of the screen and dropped a missile on the extra **C** in **CCOIN**, obliterating it.

"That is so cool," Casey whispered. "Can I play it? Have you got any coins?"

"You don't need coins," he told her with a chuckle. "I've set it to free play."

"Free play?" Pete liked the sound of that. "What do I have to do?" He jumped in front of Casey and grabbed the controls.

"Hold on. I want to show you something first," their dad said. The screen switched to a high score table. "There," he said pointing to the top position. The initials read, **MCH**. Michael Charles Henderson. The score was 17,150.

"That's you?" Pete asked, incredulous. "You're number one?"

"Yep!" Their dad blew on his fingernails and pretended to buff them on the sleeve of his fleece.

"When was the last time you played this machine?" Casey asked him.

"A long time ago…"

"And you're still at the top of the scoreboard?"

"What can I say? I was *good*."

Casey looked at her dad as if seeing him for the first time. She was impressed. "I want to know how to play like that," she said. "Teach me…"

10

DON'T TAKE ME TO
YOUR LEADER

The West Point shopping centre was in chaos. Screams echoed around the atrium as shoppers stampeded left and right, terrified by the mysterious transparent dome over the building and some unseen threat on the upper floors. Casey pushed through them, stepping over abandoned shopping bags and shards of broken glass. She looked around, trying to find her teammates and her brother. There was no sign of them.

"Pete!" she yelled. "Where are you?"

Her voice was swallowed up by the deafening hubbub. A woman pushed past, almost knocking Casey off her feet as she dragged two scared kids towards hoped-for safety in a nearby music store. Inside, Casey could see other shoppers crouched behind the racks of vinyl records. Everyone seemed terrified but she wasn't sure what of.

As she passed a stand selling cookies, a hand reached out from behind it and grabbed her wrist.

"Get down," Brain warned, pulling her to join him in a crouch. Fish was hunkered down beside him. Casey felt a wave of relief, glad not to be on her own.

"What's happening? Where are the others?"

Brain pointed to the balcony above. Several shadows were moving along it behind the glass railing. Casey's breath caught in her throat as she saw two squads of five Red Eyes moving slowly but determinedly across the balcony. Their heavy boots thudded across the marble floor like beating drums. Most of them carried plasma rifles, although one held a flickering energy sword. Its blade crackled and shimmered.

"It must be a publicity stunt," Fish whispered. But he didn't sound convinced.

Shoppers stared in shock as the soldiers approached. In their bulky, jet-black armour, the aliens dwarfed the humans around them. A couple of people held up their phones to take pictures and video for their Instagram feeds, apparently oblivious to the danger. The Red Eyes halted at a seating area. It was little more than one or two iron benches and some long-leafed ferns in raised beds. A couple of teenage girls in leggings and bomber jackets crouched beside the bushes, too scared to move.

The aliens aimed their guns and glared at them from behind their black, impenetrable helmets. A man in a baseball cap turned his phone sideways and started to video them, pinching at the screen with his fingers to get a good close-up.

"Icht refan nu," a Red Eye ordered, jerking its strange weapon at the crowd.

"What's he saying?" asked a mum holding a toddler in her arms protectively. No one knew what they were supposed to do. The teenagers by the potted plants stared helplessly, wishing they weren't so close. The only person to move was an elderly man. He pushed through the frozen crowd, tapping a walking stick in front of him. He looked about ninety with a fine trim of silver hair around a bald head.

"Who are you?" he demanded. The Red Eyes stared back at him, their eyes glowing in their helmets. "What do you want from us?"

The toddler started to cry. The Red Eyes turned as one and stared at it.

"For goodness' sake, keep your brat quiet," hissed a man dressed like a bank manager.

"He's terrified," the mum replied, jiggling the little boy on her hip. He was properly bawling now.

The elderly man took another step towards the Red Eyes until he was standing in the middle of the seating area. He balanced himself and then, slightly shakily, lifted up his walking stick and thrust it at the aliens.

"You're scaring these people," he said firmly. "Stop it."

The Red Eyes lowered their guns and, for a silly moment, Casey thought this wizened granddad had shamed them into changing their minds. Then the Red Eye carrying the energy sword stepped forwards, brushing past the potted ferns. He towered over the little old man. The other shoppers, sensing danger, started to back away.

"You don't scare me," the old man said, standing his ground. "I fought against the Nazis." He jabbed his walking stick into the alien's armoured chest. The wood clanged quietly against the metal.

In the blink of an eye, the Red Eye grabbed the old man by the throat and lifted him high into the air. His spindly legs dangled uselessly beneath him. There was a flurry of movement and Casey saw the energy sword flash. She closed her eyes, unable to watch. A moment later, she heard screams ring out and the thunder of panicked feet as the remaining shoppers fled. Then there was the terrible sound of plasma rifles firing.

This wasn't a publicity stunt.

It was real.

"I'm calling the police," Fish whispered, pulling out his phone.

"The police can't help us," Casey said, remembering the scene in the car park. "This is an invasion."

Fish's hands were shaking so much that it took him three goes to dial 999. When he finally managed it, nothing happened.

"No signal..."

"They must be blocking it," Casey said, checking her own phone's reception. It showed no bars. "There's a force field around the building. I saw it outside."

Brain looked over his shoulder at the main doors. "Can we get past it?"

Casey shook her head.

Fish flinched as more plasma fire erupted somewhere upstairs.

"It's just a game," he whispered under his breath. "It can't be real. It's just a game."

Casey ran her hands through her blue-streaked hair. They needed to find Cheeze and Elite. Most of all she had to find Pete. But she felt paralysed.

Further along the ground floor, a lift pinged open and a squad of Red Eyes stepped out. They raised their rifles and opened fire above the heads of the crowd that had gathered by the main entrance, causing a sudden stampede into the car park.

"We should move," Brain said, cautiously poking his head around the cookie stand. His voice was firm and certain, and Casey was happy for him to be in charge. He was the oldest and smartest, after all. "If we can't get outside, we need to find somewhere safe to hide. C'mon."

He broke cover and darted across the marbled floors towards the escalators. Casey and Fish followed. When they reached the moving metal staircase, they crouched low on it, staying out of sight as it carried them upwards.

The first floor was a mess. The familiar shopfronts – Boots, Home Bargains, H&M – had been shot to pieces by the Red Eyes. Fragments of broken glass and abandoned shopping bags lay scattered across the floor tiles. Scared shoppers cowered inside the shops. Casey could see the old man lying crumpled on the floor near the balcony railings. He wasn't moving. She didn't want to look too closely.

Over at the sandbagged entrance to the tournament zone, a squad of Red Eyes was pursuing a group of gamers. Casey recognized the team. They'd been in the match that played right before the Ghost Reapers took the stage. Casey had been impressed by their skill, but now they were running in terror from the aliens, freaked out by their favourite video game coming to life in front of them.

Four of the team ran into Home Bargains with the Red Eyes close behind. For some reason, the aliens didn't seem to want to shoot at them. The other gamer from their clan, an Asian kid with a pair of headphones around his neck, split sideways along the shopfront. A lone Red Eye abandoned the rest of the squad and chased him down, catching him by the scruff of his shirt and slamming him face first into the window.

Casey, too far away to help, held her breath. The Red Eye pulled a strange device like a metal loop from its belt, ripped off the gamer's headphones and began to attach the device around his neck. But before the loop could be locked in place, a security guard charged across the balcony and rugby-tackled the Red Eye, knocking the invader to one side. They smashed through the window of Home Bargains together. The Red Eye, its armour scuffed and battered from the impact, dropped its plasma rifle. The guard grabbed it and pointed it at the downed alien while the gamer stumbled away to safety, his busted headphones abandoned on the ground.

"Don't move or I'll shoot," the security guard warned.

The Red Eye got back on its feet and pulled itself up to its full height. The guard stared, his jaw dropping open. "Stay back," he warned again, trying not to let his voice betray his fear. "I mean it. Don't take another step."

The Red Eye moved forward menacingly.

The guard let out a yell that was part scream and part battle cry as he pulled the trigger on the plasma rifle. He shut his eyes as he waited for the *THWUMP!* of the weapon to kick in.

But nothing happened.

The yell died on his lips and he opened his eyes, confused. He pulled the trigger again. And again. He stared down at the gun, his hands fumbling over the weapon as he tried to work out how to use it. When he looked up again, the Red Eye was towering right over him. Its black armour now had a deep, grey scratch running across the chest plate.

The alien soldier ripped the plasma rifle from the guard's hands and then looked down at the scratch. Its eyes burned a little redder. With a swipe of its black-gloved fist, it knocked the guard off his feet. The man crumpled to the floor on a bed of broken glass, unconscious. Casey averted her eyes.

"Hey, over here!"

Behind them, a shop manager was waving at Casey from the entrance to a Tesco store. She beckoned Brain and Fish to follow and then dashed across the balcony towards the familiar red and blue logo. The security shutters were already lowering and the gamers had to duck under them to get inside before they clanged shut. Casey didn't think the shutters would do much to stop a blast of plasma fire, but it was better than nothing.

As Casey, Fish and Brain caught their breath, a familiar voice cried out behind them.

"Guys!" It was Cheeze. "Are you OK?" he asked, rolling up beside his teammates with Elite in tow.

"Only just," Fish muttered.

"Is Pete with you?" Casey asked Cheeze, her eyes darting around the store.

The boy shook his head. There was another blast of plasma fire outside.

"Those things are everywhere," a shopper said, peering through the shutters.

"What on earth are they?" asked a terrified checkout assistant.

"They're not from Earth at all," Casey said without thinking. Then she wished she hadn't spoken, as the adults stared at her questioningly. She didn't want to be the one to explain everything.

"It's like an invasion," said a middle-aged lady, still clutching a basket of ready meals as if she half-expected to finish her shopping.

"But why are they here?" wondered another. "Why aren't they outside Ten Downing Street saying, 'Take me to your leader'?"

No one had any answers. The manager stepped out in front of the crowd and raised his hands for quiet.

"Everyone, stay calm. We'll head to the back and lock ourselves in the storeroom until help comes. It's the safest place."

The other adults nodded, pleased that someone was taking charge of the situation. The Ghost Reapers looked at one another uncertainly as the shoppers began to file away.

"I don't wanna hide in no storeroom," Elite complained, staring at his trainers. "I get claustrophobic. Small spaces freak me out."

"How can the Red Eyes be real?" Cheeze whispered, glancing around the group. None of them had an answer. Finally, he turned to Casey. But she was staring at a man in a suit who had turned to follow the store manager.

"You're Lee, aren't you?" Casey said, grabbing his elbow. "You were in charge of the tournament. You must know what's going on."

Lee's brash confidence had vanished. He looked terrified. Even his suit seemed to have lost its sparkle.

"It's nothing to do with me," he said, defensively. "I just work for a brand management company." He could see from their faces that they didn't understand what that meant. "We sell merchandise and set up events like the tournament," he explained. "We don't make the actual game. We just do what they tell us."

"Who?"

"The developers, Area 51."

"And who are they?"

"I don't know. I've never met them. They do everything by email. I always thought they must be based in Poland, or Hungary. Somewhere like that. Lots of video game developers have studios in Eastern Europe. It's cheaper to hire staff."

"They authorized you to set up the eSports tournament?" Cheeze asked.

"I swear I didn't know this was going to happen," Lee whispered. "It's not my fault they took them."

"Took who?" Casey demanded. She was still holding his arm.

"The gamers, of course!" He seemed surprised they didn't already know. "A bunch of those things burst into the tournament zone after you lost your match. I told them I hadn't ordered any cosplayers. But then they pulled out their guns and started shooting. Turns out they weren't cosplayers at all."

Casey went pale. She thought of Pete out there on his own. Would the Red Eyes want to take him captive too? She should never have let him out of her sight.

"Where did they take them?" she asked, her mind racing.

Lee shook his head.

"Tell me!" Casey demanded. The forceful anger in her voice clearly surprised Lee. It surprised her even more.

"The last thing I saw, they were putting metal collars around kids' necks and leading them away, like … like prisoners," he stammered. "There wasn't anything I could do."

Casey let go of his arm. She'd gripped it so tightly that she'd crumpled the fabric of his suit. Without a backward glance, he turned and scurried after the other shoppers as they headed to the storeroom.

"Why they taking gamers prisoner?" Elite asked. "It don't make no sense."

"Experiments," Fish said, shivering slightly. "Aliens always abduct people to run experiments on them. I saw a documentary about it on the Discovery Channel."

Brain scratched his chin thoughtfully. "Maybe they're taking hostages," he suggested. "They could be using kids as a human shield while they launch their invasion."

"That's cold!" Elite cried in outrage.

"It's the only logical explanation."

Elite shook his head, annoyed by Brain's lack of emotion.

"Whatever the reason, someone's got to help them," Cheeze said. He looked to Casey for guidance, but she was lost in her own thoughts.

"What can we do against an army of Red Eyes?" Fish snapped. "You heard what they said: they're all over the shopping centre."

"We need to warn the authorities," Brain said firmly. "Tell them they're dealing with aliens."

"Not just aliens. Aliens from a video game," Elite added.

"They'll think we're nutters," Fish said, pulling

a packet of sandwiches from one of the refrigerated shelves and ripping it open. "What?" he asked as the others stared at him in surprise. "I can't think clearly when I'm hungry."

"You know that's technically looting, right?" Brain said, pointing at a security camera on the ceiling behind them.

"It's not my fault the tills are shut," Fish said petulantly, although he was careful to angle his body so the camera couldn't see his face.

"How we gonna speak to anyone anyway?" Elite asked. "We've got no phone signal. No WiFi, no 4G, no nothing."

"There's a big branch of Currys on this floor," Cheeze said. "They'll probably have a hardwired Internet connection in the computer section. Maybe it's still working. We could get the message out. I shot some video on my phone – we can upload that."

Elite fist-bumped him, impressed, then turned to Brain. "Looks like you're not the only one with brains, brainiac," he told him.

"Please stop calling me that," Brain snapped.

Casey's voice interrupted their bickering. "I've got to find Pete."

The boys suddenly felt guilty. In the chaos, they'd

totally forgotten about Casey's brother.

"We shouldn't split up," Cheeze warned her, his brow furrowing. "Besides, we need you. You're our team captain."

"She's not *my* captain," Fish said, swallowing a chunk of roast beef sandwich. "This isn't *SkyWake* any more. It's real life."

"I don't know," Brain observed, squinting through the security shutter. "It looks a lot like *SkyWake* out there to me."

"Well, even if it is, look at us," Fish said, swallowing the last of his sandwich. "We're just a bunch of gamers, not some crack military team. We need to get help and then find somewhere to hide out until the cavalry arrives. If she wants to go looking for her brother, let her. It's her fault he ran off anyway."

There was a sharp intake of breath from the rest of his team.

"Ain't right saying that, Fish," Elite scolded, his eyes narrowing.

"She lied to us," Fish reminded him, still hacked off about all that had happened earlier. "Then her brother ran away when we found out the truth. I'd say that puts it firmly on her." His face was pinched and angry.

Casey hung her head in shame. It *was* all her fault –

and now Pete was in danger because of her.

"Actually," Brain said, "we should be thanking Casey for saving us."

"Thanking me?" Casey asked, surprised. "What did I do?"

"Yeah, what did she do?" Fish demanded.

"That brand management guy said the Red Eyes attacked at the end of the tournament. If we hadn't been disqualified, we would have been there when it happened. The only reason we weren't was because of Casey. So, thinking about it logically, she saved us..."

"True dat." Elite nodded. He saw Fish glaring at him and shrugged. "What? You can't argue with logic, bruv."

"OK, then," said Brain. "Here's the plan. We'll contact the authorities and then we'll look for Pete."

Cheeze and Elite thought about this for a moment and nodded.

"Thank you," Casey said, grateful for her team's support.

"Fine," Fish muttered. "But I still don't think it's right." Then, when he was sure no one was looking, he picked up another packet of sandwiches and stuck them in his pocket for later.

11

LEVEL UP

The journey up the escalators was taking for ever. There were just too many prisoners. The Red Eye grunts and the overseers in their long cloaks were staggering the gamers, keeping them herded together on each floor and then releasing them in small batches of fifteen or so as they escorted them further up the shopping centre.

Pete was scared. He had no idea where they were going or what would happen to them when they got there. He wished he'd never run off. As he was being frogmarched alongside the other gamers, he saw shoppers hiding here and there inside the stores. The Red Eyes didn't seem to be interested in them at all.

On the third floor, the aliens stopped Pete's group outside a branch of Primark and signalled for them to wait. Plasma rifle fire echoed around the high-ceiling atrium from a floor above. It seemed like the Red Eyes were trying to clear a path ahead of them before taking the prisoners any further.

The gamers sat on the ground, their backs pressed up against the windows of the clothes store. A tall, thin boy in a red-checked lumberjack shirt, open to reveal a *SkyWake* T-shirt beneath, sniffled quietly while his friends talked among themselves in small, scared voices. A girl tapped desperately at her phone, trying to get a signal. From the snatches of conversation Pete overheard, everyone was asking the same three questions:

How can this be real?

What do they want?

What should we do?

But no one seemed to have any answers.

Pete rested against a pillar and tugged at the collar around his neck with shaking hands. It felt heavy and uncomfortable, like he was in a prison chain gang. He longed to take it off. The boy in the lumberjack shirt continued to sob. One of his teammates tried to console him.

Looking around, Pete realized that he was the only one here who wasn't part of a *SkyWake* clan. Everyone else was huddled with their teammates. Why had the Red Eyes bothered to take him? He looked down at his **COMPETITOR** badge, remembering that it had Casey's details coded onto it. Maybe they thought he was her. But what would they want with Casey? In fact, what did they want with any of the gamers?

He didn't know. He was as clueless as everyone else.

Just then he spotted a CCTV camera on the ceiling. He stared at it, wondering if someone somewhere was watching them. Someone who could help them. He raised a hand and waved at it. But the camera's lens stared back at him, motionless and indifferent. He suddenly felt stupid.

"We're going to have to make a break for it," he heard a voice say behind him. It was Xander. The boys from Strike Force were grouped outside the entrance to JD Sports. They were talking in low voices, plotting something.

"How many Red Eyes have you counted?" one of the Strike Forcers asked.

"I'm up to thirty," Xander replied. "Two overseers. The rest are grunts. They're carrying all the weapons we know from the game. Plasma and sniper rifles, shields and energy swords…"

"We don't know what these things are, though," said one of his teammates, tugging on the metal collar around his neck. "They could be explosives or anything. We need to find out before we try anything. I don't want to make a break for it and then get my head blown off."

"Hey," said Pete shyly, heading over to them. "Can I help?"

"I don't know," said the kid who'd been filming Xander earlier, "*can* you help?" His teammates chuckled at the burn. Pete felt small and useless. He was about to turn away when a sharp look from Xander made the others fall silent.

"You're Casey Flow's brother, aren't you?" the You-Tuber asked. "She with you?"

Pete shook his head. "I lost her downstairs. Maybe she got away. She's pretty fearless."

"Yeah, I noticed." Xander cast a cautious glance towards the Red Eyes. When he was sure they weren't listening, he dropped his voice low. "Are you one of my subscribers?"

"Of course," Pete replied, nodding eagerly. "I've been watching your channel since the start. I loved that thing you did where you narrated a *SkyWake* game like it was a David Attenborough nature doc."

Xander smiled thinly and looked Pete up and down. "How old are you? Thirteen? Fourteen?"

"Eleven," Pete said, beaming at having been mistaken for someone older.

"You up for helping me?"

"I'm up for anything. Anything at all."

"Great," Xander said. "Stay frosty and I'll let you know when we're ready to go."

Pete saw the other Strike Force members staring at him jealously. He sensed they didn't have much faith in him. They probably thought he was a loser. Too small, no good, couldn't even play *SkyWake* properly...

Well, he'd show them.

He could be just as good as Casey. Better, even. He just wished he didn't have this collar around his neck. He tugged at it. It felt like it was getting heavier and heavier with each passing minute.

Just then a Red Eye started kicking the prisoners sitting on the floor with its boot and jabbered something in its garbled alien tongue. It was forcing everyone back onto their feet. As the group resumed their journey through the shopping centre, Pete looked around at the gamers' miserable faces. He was secretly pleased that he knew something none of them did.

He knew that they were going to escape.

He was going to help Xander.

And he was going to be a hero.

12

"PASSWORD" IS NOT
A PASSWORD

Casey tapped the laptop to wake it up. Like all the other machines in Currys, it had gone into hibernation mode. Outside the store, the shopping centre seemed to have done the same. The earlier chaos had now been replaced by an eerie quiet. The Red Eyes had disappeared, leaving a trail of destruction in their wake, and the shoppers had taken cover wherever they could find it. The only sound was an occasional, muffled burst of plasma fire from the floors higher up.

Despite the strange calm, the team wasn't taking any chances. Elite, Brain and Fish stood guard at the entrance to the store, ready to shout if anyone – or anything – appeared.

"Damn! It needs a password!" Casey muttered as the laptop sprang back to life and a prompt appeared on-screen. She looked around the display table and even pulled out a couple of drawers, searching for a label or sticker that would help her. The drawers were full of TV remote controls, a couple of USB dongles and a busted stapler but not much else.

Cheeze rolled up beside her. "They never use strong security in shops like this," he said. "It's usually something easy for the staff to remember. Do you know what the most common password is?"

"Date of birth?"

"It's *Password*," Cheeze told her, laughing. "They use the actual word itself. Everyone thinks hackers are super-smart evil geniuses. But the truth is, most users are lazy when it comes to security."

"No wonder people get hacked all the time." Casey moved aside and let Cheeze take the keyboard.

He typed in *Password*. But it was rejected.

"Hmm," Cheeze said. "Let's rethink. How about 12345?"

He typed the numbers and hit the enter key.

"Nope. I know, let's try QWERTY, like the top row of the letters on the keyboard. People use that one all the time because it's impossible to forget."

His fingers danced over the keyboard and he hit the return key. The computer accepted it with a beep.

Casey stared at him in surprise.

"Hacker in the game, hacker in real life," he told her with a smile. "Amazing what you can teach yourself when you're sitting down all day long." He reached into one of the pouches in his wheelchair and pulled out his mobile phone and a cable and connected it to the laptop's USB port.

"Fish says who you are in real life doesn't have anything to do with the game."

"Oh, I wouldn't listen to him," Cheeze said airily. "He's got issues."

"Well, he doesn't like me much. Especially not since he found out I'm really a girl."

"Don't take it personally," Cheeze said, checking Fish couldn't overhear them. "He doesn't like anyone much at the moment. His parents split up recently and his mum went to live with another man. He's pretty cut up about it."

"How do you know about that?" Casey asked, surprised.

"We've exchanged a bunch of messages over the last few months," Cheeze explained. "It's just been him, his dad and his three brothers for a while now. I guess girls are like an alien species to him." Cheeze realized what he'd just said and rolled his eyes.

"Hmm, maybe not the best choice of words…"

He pulled up Google. "Hey, the plan is working. The phone lines must run underneath the building. I guess the force field doesn't go below the surface."

Casey thought about the drones driving themselves into the tarmac and the way the dome of light had stretched over the roof of the building. It made sense.

Cheeze logged into his Instagram account. Casey noticed that the feed was full of pictures of skateboarders.

"I used to be a skater," he told her as he clicked on the videos from the shopping centre and started to share them. "I can still do a few tricks." He raised the front wheels of his chair and spun it around in a nifty 360.

There was a ping from the laptop's speakers.

"You know, I've only got twenty followers," he said, looking a little embarrassed, "and they're all skateboard nuts. Should we send the footage to someone else? The police, newspapers, new channels?"

"Send it to all of them," Casey said. "They need to know what's happening."

Cheeze turned back to the computer and his fingers clattered over the keyboard. A moment later he stopped and stared at the newsfeed on the screen. His mouth fell open in shock.

"Looks like they're way ahead of us…"

The West Point shopping centre was all over social media and the Web. Cheeze went to the BBC News homepage, which was streaming live footage from outside the building. Sirens flashed silently all around, and military helicopters hovered in the sky above the dome.

ALIEN INVASION IN LONDON! read the caption at the bottom of the screen. The newsreader was slightly breathless, unnerved by the scale of the unfolding events. Casey watched looped footage of the scene she'd seen firsthand outside, of the police car crashing into the force field.

"Well, at least they know what's happening," Brain said, looking at the monitor. The rest of the boys had joined Casey and Cheeze in the shop, drawn to the screen by the familiar, clock-ticking theme tune. They all watched for a moment, captivated. Weirdly, seeing the shopping centre on the news made the events of the past couple of hours feel much more real.

"The authorities say they are unable to gain access to the shopping centre through what appears to be a force field," the newsreader was explaining. "As of yet there has been no contact from the invaders or any indication of what they want. Our reporter Samira Khan is at the scene."

The footage cut to a news reporter standing in the car park, microphone in hand. "Thanks, Sally. I'm here outside the shopping mall. As you can see, there's a heavy police presence and troops have started arriving. With me are some of the families of people trapped inside."

The camera panned along a crowd of worried civilians penned behind a police barricade. Casey gasped as she saw a woman in a nurse's uniform among them. The reporter shoved the microphone in her face. "Your kids are inside, aren't they? How old are they?"

"My son's eleven; my daughter's fifteen," Casey's mum said. Her voice shook. "They came here to watch a video-game tournament."

"Have the authorities told you anything?"

"Nobody's telling us anything. I just want to know they're safe." She started to cry. The reporter was about to move on to speak to someone else when Casey's mum looked up and stared straight into the camera. Her face filled the screen. "If you can hear me, kids, I love you," she said, her voice breaking. "And Casey, look after your brother. I know you will. You always do."

Then, just like that, the camera had moved on and she was gone.

In the shop, the boys all stared sympathetically at Casey as she fought back tears. She didn't want them to see her crying.

"Hey, look at these guys," Brain said, tapping the screen.

Everyone looked at the laptop. The camera had zoomed in on a group of people behind the perimeter line. They were pulling on bulky, powder-blue space-suits with huge Perspex face visors. One of the figures caught her attention.

"He was in the car park this morning," Casey said, recognizing the man with a buzz cut stepping into one of the suits.

"They look like they're coming inside," Fish said.

"I don't think that suit will be enough to get past that force field," Cheeze replied.

Before anyone could say more, they heard the sound of heavy footsteps behind them. Two Red Eyes were crossing the balcony, attracted by the sound from the laptop. The Ghost Reapers stared at one another in panic.

"Who's on look-out?" Brain demanded.

"I thought he was!" Fish said, pointing at Elite.

"You said you were!"

"Hide!" Casey hissed, ducking down beside Cheeze's wheelchair. The monitors were tall enough to cover them.

The others grabbed whatever hiding places they could find. Brain and Elite slid behind a row of washing machines. Fish crouched between two chest freezers.

The two Red Eyes stepped cautiously into the store, their guns up. They moved along the aisles of gadgets and electrical appliances, sweeping from left to right. Their heavy combat boots thudded with each step they took.

Casey recognized one of them as the alien who'd been rugby-tackled by the security guard. A deep scratch ran across its chest plate.

Elite peered around a washing machine.

"There's only two of them," he mouthed before whispering cockily, "I reckon I can take them."

"This is our first contact with an alien species," Brain hissed sharply, pushing his glasses back up his nose. "We have to try and reason with them."

"Stuff that!" Fish snapped. "Didn't you see what they did to that old guy?"

"*Shh!*" Casey warned. "They'll hear you."

"I'm gonna rush them," Elite said, ignoring her. He grabbed a fire extinguisher and brandished it like a weapon.

"No showboating," Brain warned. "We need to work together."

The Ghost Reapers held their breath as the Red Eyes continued walking through the store, towering over everything. In a few seconds they'd be right on top of them.

"What's the plan?" Casey whispered.

No one answered her. She looked at each of the boys in turn. They seemed paralysed with fear. Even Brain didn't seem to know what to do.

"Maybe they'll go away in a minute," Fish whispered, hopefully.

Casey looked at the Red Eyes. They weren't going anywhere.

She swallowed hard as the aliens continued to advance, their guns sweeping left and right across the store. It was like being hunted. Casey hesitated. She didn't want to be in charge. But someone had to do something.

The reflection of the Red Eyes' bulky shadows in the rows of TVs on display gave her an idea. She reached into the drawer of the display counter and silently grabbed the remote controls.

She held them up for the boys to see, hoping they'd understand, but the boys just stared back at her, confused.

The Red Eyes took another step closer.

Casey jabbed the button on the first remote and a TV across the store turned on at full volume. A footballer had just scored a winning goal on-screen and the cheers of the crowd erupted from the speakers. It was loud.

The Red Eyes turned in surprise and opened fire together. They blasted the TV into pieces. Smoke billowed out.

Casey jabbed the other remotes in quick succession and TVs and hi-fi systems all across the store switched themselves on one by one. Convinced they were under attack, the aliens began firing left and right.

"Push the fridges!" Casey yelled, running towards a row of tall, American-style fridge-freezers near the aliens.

With Brain and Fish's help, she shoved the first fridge over and it crashed into the one beside it, setting off a cascade as the appliances toppled like dominoes.

The last fridge in the row, a cream SMEG, crashed onto both Red Eyes, knocking them off balance.

One of the aliens hit the floor, trapped under the fridge. Elite sprayed its helmet with the fire extinguisher, covering its red eyes under a layer of thick foam.

As it thrashed around blindly, Casey leaped forwards and scooped up its dropped plasma rifle. The other Red Eye, knocked off balance by the trap but still standing, let out a roar of anger and opened fire just as Casey ducked down a side aisle between some washing machines.

She headed for the doors, plasma searing through the air around her. Toasters and tumble dryers exploded as the Red Eye released a pitiless barrage of fire. Casey half ran, half stumbled towards the entrance, hoping to draw its attention away from her friends, who were still crouched between the fridges and the trapped Red Eye covered in white foam.

"Run!" she yelled. "I'll distract it."

The alien with the scratched armour lumbered after her, its heavy boots pounding the floor. Its red eyes seemed to narrow as it acquired her as a target.

Her plan was working!

She put her head down and sprinted out of the

front of the shop. She just hoped the boys would make the most of their chance to escape.

13

SHAKE AND BAKE

As she sprinted through the shopping centre, Casey passed the sandbagged doorway to the tournament zone. It seemed like a lifetime ago that she'd been in there playing *SkyWake*. Now here she was being chased by a real-life Red Eye while clutching an enormous plasma rifle. The gun felt big in her hands, and was incredibly heavy. She didn't know how much longer she could hold it.

Looking around for somewhere to hide, she darted towards a nearby kitchenware shop. As she approached, the security shutters were rolling down, blocking off the entrance. She stuck her fingers through the gaps in the shutters and rattled it, shouting at the people inside as they hid among chopping boards, blenders and dinner sets.

"Let me in," she begged. "Please let me in."

The shoppers stared back at her in fright.

"We didn't shut them," said a woman in a long, flowery skirt. "It must be some kind of automatic thing."

Casey looked around. It was true. All the other shutters on this floor seemed to be descending. She pulled at the metal barrier in front of her desperately, and several people inside the store did the same on the other side.

It was hopeless. The shutters wouldn't move.

"It's right behind me," Casey said, panting for breath.

"You have to run," the woman advised. "Those things are rounding up all you gamers. We saw them. They're not interested in anyone else. Just the players."

"What are they doing to them?"

"They took a bunch of them upstairs. They looked like prisoners."

Casey's vision swam as she realized what that meant. Was Pete upstairs too? She had to go after him.

The woman stared through the shutter at the strange alien weapon in Casey's hands.

"Get out of here," she told her. "Save yourself."

Casey nodded and fled, sprinting along the marble floors until she saw a Starbucks further along the balcony. It was the one she'd met her teammates in earlier that morning. Something about its familiarity was comforting. She slammed through its doors.

She was safe … for now.

The coffee shop had been abandoned in haste. Mugs and half-eaten muffins were left on the tables. Upturned chairs lay on the floor. The coffee machine behind the baristas' counter hissed and thudded, full of steam that needed to be released.

Casey darted between the tables and ran towards the back of the café, hoping to find a rear exit, but there wasn't one. The only door she found led into the toilets.

Behind her, through the shop window, she could see the lone Red Eye searching the food court outside. The alien moved slowly and deliberately, the shopping centre's bright lights reflecting off its scratched black suit.

Scratch, she thought. *That's a good name for him.* She had decided it was a "him", although she couldn't actually see who or what was inside the bulky combat suit.

Crouching low in the mouth of the corridor that led to the toilets, she considered hiding in the ladies'.

Maybe Scratch wouldn't search in there. But the idea made her nervous. Once she went in she'd be trapped with no way out.

She didn't want to die in a toilet.

She didn't want to die full stop. But she definitely didn't want to die in a toilet.

She looked at the plasma rifle still in her hands. It was a strange shade of silvery grey, like it was made of graphite. There was an instrument panel on its side, a touchscreen about the size of an iPhone. She let her fingers brush against the touchscreen and the weird alien glyphs glowed as they sensed the proximity of her skin.

She stared at them, suddenly realizing they were familiar.

And that was when it hit her.

They were exactly like the ones in *SkyWake*. She'd seen this control panel a million times before in the game. Her avatar's fingers had moved over it every time she reloaded. She knew the sequence off by heart.

She tapped the glyphs in the order needed to ready the gun. There was a low-frequency hum as the weapon drew power from its battery packs. Casey felt her skin tingle as the electrons in the air around her were charged with energy.

If this gun worked like the rifles in the game, she knew exactly how to use it.

There was a crash as Scratch banged open the doors and stepped into the café. He looked around the empty store suspiciously, his black armour silhouetted against the window.

As Casey watched, his helmet shot out a lattice of red scanning lasers. They roved over the abandoned shop, moving across the tables and overturned chairs. She wasn't sure if the scanner was tracking body heat or looking for signs of movement. Or maybe it was some advanced alien tech that she couldn't even begin to comprehend. She ducked back around the corner, trying to stay hidden. She wanted to scream or run away. Doing either would mean instant death.

The scanner moved methodically, searching every inch of the café, slowly making its way towards her hiding place. She flattened herself against the wall as the laser beam approached. It was no good. It was going to find her.

She wondered what lay behind the alien's helmet. Was it anything like a human face? Could he feel compassion? Could she reason with him? Would he hesitate to pull the trigger if he saw that she was just a scared teenager?

Somehow she didn't think so.

You're going to die in here, she thought to herself.

Casey swallowed hard, wishing she had some water to soothe the dry itch in her throat. She couldn't remember the last time she'd had anything to drink. Her hands trembled as they gripped the plasma rifle. She felt the same tremor building in her legs. She wished she could just run away, but there was nowhere to run.

She had to fight.

She stepped out of her hiding place with the stock of the plasma rifle pressed against her shoulder. Her muscles screamed at the weight of it but she knew she couldn't drop it. She pressed her cheek against the metal side, feeling it cool against her skin, and lined up Scratch in her holographic sights.

He hadn't spotted her yet.

"Looking for me?" she asked loudly. She wasn't sure why she said it, but there in that moment it made her feel like she was the heroine of a blockbuster movie. One of those sassy, whip-smart girls who always know the right thing to say, no matter how bad things get.

She felt her finger curl around the trigger as Scratch turned to face her. The firing mechanism was stiff and heavy and it took all her strength to pull back on it. Even when the trigger moved, it seemed to take for ever to do anything. She felt the tremor building in her hands and arms and …

… *FWUUUMMMMPPPHH!* The rifle's barrel filled with energy and shot out a bright green streak of plasma. The recoil from the gun took her by surprise, almost ripping the weapon out of her grip. The barrel jerked upwards, sending her shot wide of its target. The plasma burst smashed into the wall behind the baristas' station and sliced through the brickwork, creating a perfect circle. Through it she could see a pizza restaurant next door.

Casey's body sagged as she realized that she'd missed. Scratch shifted his weight slightly and turned to stare at it too. It was impossible to know what he was thinking behind his expressionless helmet. She guessed he wasn't happy. She had just tried to kill him after all.

"Um…" Casey muttered, letting the plasma rifle drop beside her leg.

"*Rth'he calfu mort,*" the alien droned, his mechanical eyes burning bright red. His voice sounded flat and insulting, as if he was saying, *You should have aimed better, you stupid girl.*

"Yeah," Casey agreed with a thin grimace. "I guess you're right."

Scratch lifted his rifle onto her. At that moment, Casey knew that she was going to die in Starbucks in the West Point shopping centre. It didn't seem like a very fitting end to her fifteen years of life.

Still, at least it wasn't a toilet.

Scratch's plasma rifle hummed and glowed, and then it fired.

THWUMP!

Casey felt the room moving around her. It took a moment to realize what was happening. It wasn't the room that was moving, it was her!

She had no memory of making a decision to dive. It just kind of happened. It was as though her body had taken over from her mind, leaving all her usual doubts and uncertainty behind. She found herself flying through the air as the plasma blast ripped towards her. She landed, with a thud, face down on the floorboards behind the counter with the plasma rifle underneath her. It jabbed into her ribs, winding her.

She might have passed out if it hadn't been for another massive *THWUMP!* above her head as a second blast of plasma seared through the thick wooden counter. She felt its burning heat on her scalp.

The coffee machine released a hiss of pent-up steam and then exploded. Roasted coffee beans and shards of broken mugs were thrown into the air.

Casey crawled along the floor behind the counter, stomach flat on the ground. A third blast from the plasma rifle ate into another section of the counter, chipping away at her cover. She knew there was no way she could stand and return fire.

What should she do?

Her fingers were already tapping her own plasma rifle's touchscreen. She was halfway through the sequence before her mind caught up with them.

"Shake and bake," she whispered to herself.

In *SkyWake* it was possible to turn a plasma rifle into a makeshift bomb by overcharging its battery pack. If you were really lucky you could take out the whole enemy team with it. But if you timed the "shake and bake" wrong by even a fraction of a second, you'd blow yourself up. A lot of *SkyWake* players thought shaking and baking was an exploit, an unintended bug in the code that gamers were able to use for their advantage. Casey wasn't so sure. Shaking and baking was so crazy it felt like it must have been intentional. It was a lunatic strategy, the kind of thing you had to be both fearless *and* stupid to try.

Well, Casey though to herself, *I guess I never was all that clever.*

She watched as the glyphs glowed beneath her fingers. The rifle began to hum and crackle as it overcharged. In the game, all you had to do was hit a key to throw it. In real life, it was going to be harder. The rifle was as heavy as a sack of potatoes.

She took a deep breath and stood up behind what was left of the wooden counter.

"I surrender," she said, cradling the plasma rifle in her arms like a giant metal baby. Scratch trained his gun on her again.

"Han flecht na daruda!" he shouted, nodding at the weapon in her hands. She guessed he was telling her to put it down.

"Sure," Casey told him, "you can have it. I don't need it any more."

With that, she gathered all her strength and threw the plasma rifle over the counter into the coffee shop. It landed on the floor among the overturned tables and chairs. Scratch grunted, satisfied, and took a step towards her. As he did, he noticed the flashing touchscreen on the side of her rifle. He stared at it for a second, his eyes glowing an even darker shade of red. Maybe it was just her imagination, but for a moment

Casey was convinced they looked scared.

She didn't wait to see the explosion. She heard and felt the blast as she ducked back down behind the cupboards. The rifle's battery pack lit up the coffee shop like a firework, filling the air with searing heat. When Casey was sure it was over, she cautiously stood back up again.

Scratch had been thrown halfway across the store by the blast. The air around him crackled with electrical energy. Casey ran over to where he lay on the floor.

"Where's my brother?" she demanded.

Scratch turned his head to look at her. He didn't respond. Casey wasn't even sure he knew what she was saying. Did he understand the word "brother"? Did they even have families where he was from? She wished she could see what was underneath the curved black helmet.

She reached down to pick up Scratch's plasma rifle, to replace the one she'd just turned into a bomb. It was battered from the blast but still working. It might come in useful before today was over. As she took it, the alien grabbed her wrist with his black-gloved hand. Casey stared into his burning red eyes for a second then pulled herself free.

"Game over," Casey said in her best blockbuster heroine voice. Then she turned and ran out of the café.

She only managed to take a few steps before she had to stop and throw up.

14

GO WITH THE FLOW

Space Invaders was simple to play but hard to master. Standing in the garage, Casey and Pete took it in turns. The aim was to stop five rows of blocky invading aliens from reaching the bottom of the screen. The only weapon you had was a gun turret that slid left and right below them. When things got too much, you could hide from the aliens' missiles under one of four chunky bases. But the bases slowly disintegrated as they were hit.

Space Invaders didn't have a story. You didn't know who the aliens were or why they were invading. You just had to stop them. Every time you cleared a screen of enemies, though, a new wave of invaders appeared that was faster and more deadly than before. It was frustrating, yet addictive.

"I hate this game," Pete complained as his gun turret

blew up for the hundredth time that day. "There's no way to win."

"You're not supposed to win," his dad laughed. "These old arcade games were designed to make you lose so you'd keep slotting in more coins. Why don't you have another go? I'll help you this time."

Dad watched as Pete played, studying his moves and giving him tips.

"The game came from Japan," he explained. "The designer based the aliens on sea creatures. Those ones at the top look like squids. They're worth thirty points. That one over there is a crab. It's twenty points. This one's an octopus. He'll get you ten points." He pointed to the pixel enemies as they stuttered across the screen. "When *Space Invaders* was first released, it was so popular that the whole of Japan ran out of coins."

"You're putting me off," Pete whined, as he lost the first of his three lives.

"I was just trying to teach you something," their dad said softly. Casey could see that Pete wasn't interested. A couple of minutes later, Pete lost his last life.

"I don't know why you bought this piece of junk," he moaned.

"I just wanted you to see what video games were like when I was your age."

"Well, now I know. They were crap."

"Peter!"

"I'm gonna go play *Fortnite*." Pete pushed past Casey and headed back into the house.

"He never likes being told what to do, does he?" their dad mused. "Always thinks he's more grown up than he actually is." He turned to Casey. "What about you? Are you bored of it too?"

"No way." Casey stepped up to the machine. She was secretly pleased to have her dad all to herself. He watched her as she cleared the first couple of screens. On every new screen, the invaders got faster and faster. The thudding sound effects sped up too. It reminded her of the theme tune for *Jaws*.

Duh-dah. Duh-dah. Duh-dah. Duh-dah. Duh-dah. Duh-dah. Duh-dah.

It was surprisingly stressful.

"Concentrate your fire on the column on the right," her dad advised after she'd lost two of her lives. Casey blasted the column he pointed to, wiping them out. It was a great strategy. By removing the column, you added a second or two to the invaders' journey across the screen, slowing them down before they descended to the next row.

"Nicely done," her dad said encouragingly. "Try not to think too much. Just let your hands take over. Move. Stop. Shoot."

A siren wailed as a flying saucer moved across the top of the screen. Casey knew it was worth bonus points if she could hit it. She scooted out from under a base and tried to line up her shot.

"No!" she yelped as her turret took a direct hit from an alien missile. She looked at her score.

"Not bad," her dad said.

"It's nowhere near your high score."

He stroked his chin thoughtfully. "You know what your problem is, Casey? You're thinking too much. You need to find your flow."

"Flow? What's that?"

"It's what they call it when you're in the zone," he explained. "When you get really good at some-thing – really, really good – your mind empties and your instincts take over. You stop worrying about everything and just exist in the moment. When a professional musician gets onstage, he doesn't think about how to play. He just plays. It's automatic. Or when an Olympic runner hears the starting pistol, she isn't thinking about how to run. She just runs. Or…"

His voice trailed off.

"Or what?" Casey asked, sensing something interesting behind his hesitation.

"Nothing."

"Come on, Dad. Tell me."

He paused a moment, as if deciding whether or not to finish his thought. She gave him her best puppy-dog expression. He sighed.

"I was going to say that it's like when I'm defusing a bomb."

Casey looked at him sideways. He hardly ever talked about his job with her.

"When someone finds an unexploded bomb in a war zone, they call my team in to help," he explained. "By the time we get there, the local police and the army have usually cleared the area and pulled everyone back to a safe distance. I put on my bomb suit and helmet and walk into the evacuated area. It's completely still and quiet. We call it the Long Walk."

Casey listened silently, not wanting to say anything in case he stopped. "As you make that walk, your mind just empties. Nothing else matters. It's just you and the bomb. You're totally focussed on defusing that thing without it exploding."

"Aren't you scared?"

"Of course I am. But I can't listen to that little voice in the back of my head saying, *Run away!* or, *You're going to die!* I have to block it out to get the job done."

"You have that voice too?" she asked, surprised. She often heard a whiny voice telling her she was no good.

"Everyone does," he laughed. "The trick is to learn how to ignore it."

Casey felt strange. Hearing her dad talking about dying had freaked her out. He must have sensed her discomfort because he changed the subject quickly.

"Let's try again," he said, tapping the start button. "But this time, go with the flow…"

On the last Saturday night of the summer holidays, the family shared a Chinese takeaway. While Casey and Pete fought over the last barbecue spare rib, their dad announced that he was being deployed again.

"We're leaving on Wednesday," he said. "Someone made a mistake with our orders. It's all a bit last-minute."

Casey felt the temperature in the room drop. Her mum toyed with the noodles in her bowl.

"I'm sorry, Rebecca. I know it's not long to prepare."

Casey looked from one parent to the other and waited for her mum to say something. It was Pete who spoke first, though.

"You're going to miss my birthday," he said quietly, almost under his breath. He was turning nine in two weeks and had asked for a paintball party in the woods. Dad had promised to put him and all his mates through "basic training".

"We'll work something out. Why don't we celebrate your birthday early?"

"Will we still be able to go paintballing?"

"I don't think we can move the party," their mum said. "But your dad's right, we'll sort something else out. An extra birthday surprise. Just the four of us."

Casey could see her mum was upset. She wasn't even looking at her dad as she spoke.

Pete pushed away from the table. "I thought you said the war was over."

"It is," Dad told him, "but we still have soldiers out there, trying to make the country safe for the people who live there. It's important."

"It's not fair," Pete said crossly. "You said you'd be here."

"I'm really sorry, son. It isn't my choice."

"You've spent all summer playing that stupid game

with Casey. What about me? When do I get to do something special with you?"

Dad looked hurt. "How about we find something we can do together when I get back?" he suggested. "What about that old Nintendo 64 console we saw on eBay? I'll teach you how to play *GoldenEye*. You'll love it. We can play deathmatch, all three of us."

"I don't want to play all three of us!" Pete shouted. "I just want you to play with *me*. If you loved me you would be here." He rushed out of the room and thundered up the stairs.

"He doesn't mean it, Mike," Casey's mum said. "He's just upset."

"Does he really think I want to miss his birthday?" their dad asked softly. "Doesn't he understand that I don't get a choice about when we leave?"

"I know. Let me talk to him."

In the kitchen, a little later, Casey washed the dishes while her dad dried them with a tea towel. She rinsed suds off a bowl and passed it to him.

"Why do you keep going back if you're scared?" she blurted out. "Why don't you just stay here with us and Mum?"

Her dad stopped drying the bowl. "Because it's my job."

"You could get another one."

They stood in silence a moment.

"I joined the Royal Engineers because I wanted to help people," her dad told her. "My team goes to dangerous places and we try and stop people from getting killed by bombs, IEDs, anything that goes *ka-boom!*"

"Mum's angry with you."

"No, she's just worried. She always worries about me when I'm away. It's a dangerous job … but it's what I've been trained to do."

Her dad finished drying the bowl and put it away in the cupboard.

"Do you know what scares me more than being blown up?" he asked. "Letting my team down. There's four other people in my squad and I'm in charge of them. They're my responsibility. They all have families who care about them too. That's why I have to go. I have to look after them."

"Why you? Can't someone else do it?"

"Because I'm good at what I do, Casey. It's the only thing I've ever been really good at."

"Apart from video games," said Casey. "You're good at them, too."

Her dad didn't say anything.

Casey scraped leftover noodles into the food waste

and then washed up the plate.

"Is leading people hard, Dad?" she asked.

He stopped to think about the question before he answered it.

"It's a lot of responsibility. The trick is to believe in yourself. Because if you don't, how will anyone else?"

Casey passed him the wet plate to dry. "It's like *Space Invaders*," she said, thoughtfully. "You're responsible for keeping everyone safe."

Her dad put down the plate and gave her a big hug. He held her tight in his strong arms and she pretended not to see the tears in his eyes.

"Right then," he said when he'd collected himself, "these dishes aren't going to wash themselves."

Casey didn't realize it, but that would be the last conversation she'd have with her dad.

15

PRESS BUTTON TO
SPEAK TO OPERATOR

Casey ran for the lifts. Her arms ached from holding Scratch's plasma rifle, but she didn't dare put it down. She could hear footsteps in the distance through the eerie silence of the shopping centre. The Red Eyes were hunting her.

She jabbed the button anxiously. The lift began its slow descent towards her.

Fourth floor. Third floor.

It was in no hurry.

Casey wondered what she'd do if the lift was full of aliens. She couldn't take on a whole squad of them. This was nothing like the game. In *SkyWake* you had a team and you worked together, and even if you failed, it didn't really matter. Your dinner would still be on the table after you logged out, and your friends would still be waiting for you at school the next day.

It wasn't real.

Here in the shopping centre, though, it was life and death … with no respawns.

She stared at her watch. It had been almost an hour since the attack began. Which meant it had been an hour since she had last seen Pete. She remembered what the woman in the kitchenware shop had said about the Red Eyes taking prisoners. She had to find her brother. But how? On an ordinary day she'd go and ask for an announcement on the public address system. Or find a security guard. She looked up at the ceiling, noticing a camera.

That was it! The CCTV system.

If she could find the security control room, she could use the cameras to hunt for Pete.

The lift pinged, jolting her out of her thoughts. She tensed … but it was empty. She jumped inside and hit the button for the floor above.

"Doors closing," said a robotic voice.

Along the balcony she could hear footsteps coming her way. They were running at full pelt now, pounding the marble floor tiles. The Red Eyes had found her!

She jabbed the up button again, faster this time. The mechanism was so slow.

The doors began to close. She willed them to hurry

but they slid towards one another without any sense of urgency.

The footsteps drew closer and closer.

Casey instinctively dropped to one knee and adopted a firing position. She stared down the rifle's sights, aiming at the closing gap between the lift doors. Holding the gun like that, seeing nothing but the barrel and her hands, was like being in first-person mode. She held her breath. The doors had almost closed when a foot jammed them open. They jerked apart again automatically.

Casey's finger tightened around the trigger.

"Don't shoot!" yelled Brain, pulling up short and throwing his hands over his face in shock as he saw the gun pointing at him. Elite skidded into his back.

Casey let the rifle drop. Her stomach lurched as she realized how close she'd come to blasting her friends. The two boys bundled inside the lift, falling over one another in their haste.

"They're right behind us!" Brain said.

"Where are the others?"

"We got split up," Elite explained, panting for breath. His tracksuit was ripped and his once brilliant-white trainers were now scuffed and dirty. "It was nasty. The Red Eyes were shooting everything."

"We can't just leave them behind," Casey said.

It was too late. Just before the doors slid together, Casey glimpsed four Red Eyes come running around the corner. Then the doors clanged shut. They were safe. For now.

"Lift going up."

The boys stared in awe at the plasma rifle in Casey's hands.

"Do you know how to use that thing?" Brain asked.

Casey turned the rifle onto its side to show them the touchscreen with its familiar glyphs.

"It's just like in the game," she explained.

"What, like, press 'X' to reload?" Elite scoffed, incredulous.

Before Casey could explain further, the lift jerked violently to a stop, almost knocking them off their feet.

"What happened?" she asked. "Did they cut the power?"

"The lights are still on," Brain said, looking up. It was true. The lift's lights hadn't even flickered. It was the mechanism that had stopped.

"Small spaces freak me out big time," Elite fretted, eyeing the walls as if they were about to close in on them. He bunched his hands into fists over and over.

Casey looked at Brain, uncertain what to do.

"Hey, you guys," said a voice. It seemed to come out of thin air.

"Who said that?" Brain demanded, looking around suspiciously.

"Over here," the voice said. It wasn't the lift's robotic tone. It was a real person speaking to them. Casey followed the sound to the lift's control panel. "That's it," the voice encouraged them. It was as if it could see them.

"Cheeze?" Casey asked, suddenly recognizing their friend's voice. There was no answer. She could see a circular speaker built into the control panel. There was an embossed sign above it: IN AN EMERGENCY, PRESS BUTTON TO SPEAK TO OPERATOR.

Casey hit the button. It was stiff from lack of use.

"Cheeze?" she asked. "Is that you?" The voice was silent. "Hello?" Nothing. She released the button. As soon as she did, the speaker on the panel burst back into life with a crackle.

"You need to let go of the button to hear me," the voice said. "It's like a walkie-talkie, not a telephone."

"Cheeze!" Casey shouted, thrilled. "It *is* you! Where are you? Can you help us get moving? The lift is stuck." She remembered to release the button this time.

"I've got some good news and some bad news," Cheeze told them. "Bad news is there's a bunch of Red Eyes waiting on the next floor. They look like they're going to ambush you."

"You can see them?"

"I can see everything," Cheeze said, showing off a little. "Smile, you're on camera." Casey looked up at the ceiling and noticed a fish-eye CCTV lens staring down at them. "Me and Fish are in the security control room," he explained.

"Please, guys," Elite interrupted. "I just want to get out of here. There's no air. I feel like I'm suffocating." His back slid down the wall until he was sitting on the floor with his knees against his chest. His breathing came shallow and fast.

"Can we get the lift moving again?" Casey asked Cheeze, jabbing buttons at random.

"I overrode it to keep you safe," Cheeze told her. "The Red Eyes are everywhere."

"So what's the good news?" Brain asked, reaching past Casey to hold the button in, then letting go.

"We found a map of the building in the control room. There's a hatch in the roof of the lift. If you can get out of it, you should be able to climb the service ladder up the shaft. About a floor and a half above you there's an air vent. Get inside it and you can crawl through the ventilation system to us."

"No way," Elite moaned from the floor. "I ain't crawling through no vents."

"How sure are you about this?" Brain asked.

Casey could imagine Cheeze's shrug from the tone of his voice.

"Not very," he said. "But unless you want to stay in the lift, it's the only option."

Casey exchanged a concerned look with Brain. "I've got to find Pete," she said. Then she looked up at the roof, seeing the outline of the hatch set into it. She slung the plasma rifle over her back. "Give me a boost."

Casey poked her head through the hatch and pulled herself up. The air was stale and cold. She was relieved to see that there were only a few centimetres between the concrete walls of the shaft and the side of the lift. It meant there was no way to fall. That was something, at least.

She looked up, following the huge steel cable that held the lift. It stretched into the shadows above her in a giant loop. At regular intervals along the walls of the shaft she could see the metal doors where the lift would stop to let people in and out. A service ladder, little more than some metal rungs embedded into the concrete, ran up one side. She followed its ascent, craning her neck as she peered into the darkness. It went so far up it made her feel dizzy.

"I've found the ladder," she told the boys as she poked her head back through the hatch. Brain grabbed her hand and she pulled him up. Elite didn't move. He stayed on the floor, hugging his knees.

"I can't do it," he said without looking up.

"We'll help you," Casey said gently.

"I ain't going," he muttered, rocking backwards and forwards. "No way. Forget it."

"We'll have to just leave him behind," Brain whispered to Casey.

"What if the lift restarts? He'll have no chance against the aliens on his own."

"What's taking you so long?" Cheeze's voice said, crackling through the control panel's tinny speaker. "Why isn't Elite moving? Is he hurt?"

Casey dropped back through the hatch and crouched down beside Elite. She wished she knew his real name. Calling him by his gamertag seemed like an insult when the normally cocky sniper was now feeling far from elite.

"Elite, we need to get out of here. It's not safe."

"I can't do it," he whined. His usual bragging confidence had melted away. "When I was little, my gran used to lock me under the stairs for misbehaving. She was fierce, yo. Proper old-school. I can't stand small spaces no more…"

He wiped the sleeve of his tracksuit over his wet cheeks, embarrassed. Casey touched his arm gently.

"I'm scared too. But you know who's more scared than both of us?"

Elite looked up at her.

"My little brother. He's out there on his own. I need to get to him. But I can't do it without you."

"I ain't no use to you," Elite sniffled. "I just can't do it."

Brain stuck his head back in through the roof hatch. We need to be logical about this. If he doesn't want to come, we can't make him."

"We can't leave him, either," Casey snapped. She turned back to the boy in the lift. "The Elite Sniper I know isn't afraid of anything," she told him. "He charges into trouble head first, always showboating, always clicking heads."

"Yeah, but that's in the game," Elite snivelled. "In real life, I get beaten up on the 178 bus by the Year

Elevens for spitting second-rate rhymes. Real life ain't nothing like the game."

"Isn't it?" Casey asked, motioning to the plasma rifle slung on her back.

Elite buried his head in his knees. "I can't do it," he repeated. "Go without me."

"Casey," Brain hissed impatiently from the roof. "We don't have time."

She hesitated, torn. She felt responsible for Elite. He was her teammate. She couldn't just leave him. But she also knew she had to find Pete – she had to make sure he was safe.

"You're not doing it," she whispered to Elite. His pale, lean face looked up at her. "*We're* doing it. Together. That's what being in a team is all about. We watch each other's backs. You feel me, bruv?" She held out her hand.

Elite smiled, despite himself, at her imitation of him. He hesitated a moment then reached out and took it.

"I feel you," he said as she hauled him to his feet. "For real."

There was a crackle from the speaker in the control panel.

"We've got a problem," Cheeze's voice hissed.

"You need to get out of there. Now!"

Before anyone could respond, the lift jolted back into life and started to climb upwards again. Whatever override Cheeze had put in place seemed to have timed out.

"Quick!" Casey yelled, bundling Elite towards the roof hatch. He jumped and pulled himself up, his trainers kicking the empty air as he wriggled through. Once he was clear, Casey leaped for the hatch, but she wasn't tall enough to make it through without a boost.

"Grab my hand," Brain shouted as he reached down through the hole. Elite appeared beside him and did the same.

Casey jumped. She missed their outstretched hands. Behind her there was a *ping!*

"Doors opening."

She took another leap and the boys heaved her up through the hatch. They didn't even have time to close it before a Red Eye appeared in the now open doorway and stepped inside. His bulky black armour filled the narrow lift compartment and the energy sword in his hand crackled ominously as he looked around.

Standing on the roof of the lift, Casey and the

boys pressed themselves against the concrete walls of the lift shaft. If the Red Eye looked up, he'd spot them. Casey imagined him running his energy sword through the roof of the lift. In the game, the energy blades were perfect for cutting through metal. They could slide right through fifteen centimetres of steel as if it was a sheet of kitchen foil. Her hands tightened around the plasma rifle. Would she even have time to fire off a shot before he skewered them?

The Red Eye shifted his weight slightly and cocked his head. He seemed to be admiring his reflection in the mirror on the back wall of the lift. Then he adjusted his helmet slightly, grunted and stepped out.

"Doors closing."

Casey looked at the boys and all three of them remembered to breathe again.

"Just as well we didn't leave you behind," Brain whispered to Elite, patting him on the shoulder before turning to Casey. There was new-found respect in his eyes. "That's the second time you've saved us today, Casey Flow."

Casey wasn't listening. All she could think about was finding her little brother. She looked up at the service ladder that stretched into the shadows above them.

"Let's keep moving," she ordered as she reached out to grab the first rung. "And whatever you do, don't look down."

16

A SHOCKING DEVELOPMENT

Pete had never been on the eighth floor of the West Point building before, although he'd always wanted to. It was home to a multiplex cinema, a ten pin bowling alley and a gym and sauna. There were even rumours that there was an open-air rooftop pool. Looking around, though, he couldn't see any sign of it. Maybe it was just a myth.

There were no shoppers or staff on this floor. The aliens had cleared the place out and turned it into a temporary base. Fixed energy shields, shaped like clam-shells, stood at the top of the escalators. It looked like the Red Eyes were digging in, ready to stop an attack.

Perhaps, Pete thought with a sudden burst of hope, the authorities had realized what was happening. Maybe they were about to send in a rescue team. At any moment, SAS soldiers would abseil down the building and storm in and rescue him.

Pete watched a squad of Red Eyes arming themselves from some purple supply crates containing weapons and ammo. He wasn't sure how well even the SAS would fare against Arcturian plasma rifles.

The aliens shoved the captured gamers through a set of double doors marked STAFF ONLY. They led into a service corridor. The gamers marched along it and up a concrete stairwell.

Trudging up the steps, Pete wondered when Xander was going to act. Despite all his bravado, the YouTuber had yet to actually make a move. Maybe he didn't have a plan. Or maybe he did and he had simply decided that Pete wasn't worth including in it.

At the top of the stairwell, a door opened and the gamers stepped out onto the roof of the shopping mall. On an ordinary day they might have stared in wonder at the impressive urban sprawl stretching out in all directions. But today was no ordinary day.

Instead, their gasp was prompted by the incredible sight of an Arcturian dropship perched on the roof on its enormous landing gear. It was fully decloaked and its wings stretched over their heads, casting the roof in shadow. Standing there, their necks craning to look up at it, the awestruck gamers looked like visitors to the Sistine Chapel marvelling at its famous ceiling.

"Whoa!" the video kid whispered, lifting his camera to film it all. "It's like something out of a … a…" His voice trailed off, unable to finish his sentence.

"A video game?" Pete suggested, overcome by a fit of nervous giggles. They quickly stopped as a Red Eye shoved him hard between the shoulder blades, forcing him onwards with the butt of his plasma rifle.

As Pete stumbled forwards, he noticed the energy dome surrounding the shopping centre and stretching over the top of the dropship. They were completely sealed inside. Beyond the curve of the dome, three Apache attack helicopters hovered in the sky. They looked like toys beside the dropship.

The prisoners were shepherded across the rooftop. Two Red Eyes stood on either side of a loading ramp that hung beneath the dropship's undercarriage, scanning the gamers as they entered. The whole process was slick and efficient. The Arcturians were infamous for their ruthless organization and imperial ambition. Not for nothing did *SkyWake* players called them the Romans of outer space. They loved rules and order, which was part of the reason why they hated the Squids with their mysterious telepathic powers.

As the gamers shuffled forwards, Pete saw that they were being kept in their clans. Each team – including Xander and the rest of Strike Force in their distinctive eSports jerseys – was kept separate from the others.

With a sudden chill he wondered what that meant for him. He was the only one here who wasn't part of a clan. He was the stray, the spare wheel, the misfit. He imagined the scanners beeping angrily as they ran over his face.

Reject. Reject. Reject.

There was a ripple of activity up ahead. He watched as each gamer turned and whispered something to the person behind. Pete realized that a message was being passed along. He watched its progress until it finally reached the boy in front of him. It was the video kid from Strike Force. The lanky boy turned his head and, checking the Red Eyes weren't watching, spoke quickly over his shoulder.

"Tell Pete to create a distraction," he said, then snapped his head back to face the front. Pete nodded and turned around, ready to pass on the message to the gamer behind him.

"Tell Pete to create a dis—" he began. Then he realized his mistake. There was no one behind him.

He was Pete. Which meant it was his job to create a distraction.

He gulped. The line shuffled forwards.

Well, he thought to himself, *this is your chance to prove yourself.*

He looked around at the Red Eyes on the rooftop. There were four grunts and one hooded overseer. The overseer was the only one without a weapon. Pete reckoned he'd have to be quick to get to him before the grunts had a chance to lift their plasma rifles.

He paused, letting his brain do the maths. He saw Xander staring at him expectantly. The YouTuber flashed him his trademark "X" with his index fingers.

Pete nodded.

This was his moment to show Xander what he was made of. Counting down in his head – three, two, one! – he bent low and made a run for it, charging so close to the overseer that he made the ends of the alien's long black cloak twitch.

Then he jumped onto the sloping bank of solar panels, hooting and hollering like a maniac in an attempt to get all the Red Eyes to look in his direction. The overseer tried to grab him but missed, and Pete slid across the panels like a surfer on a wave. Any moment now he expected to hear the sound of the gamers charging forwards under Xander's command. But there was nothing but silence.

He looked over his shoulder and saw, with surprise, that no one had moved a muscle. They all just stood and stared at him as if he was an idiot. The overseer reached under the folds of his cloak and pulled out a device that looked like a TV remote control. He pressed a button.

Bzzzzt! Pete felt his body tense with searing pain. His jaw clamped together and his spine arched backwards as the shackle around his neck pumped electrical energy into him. He hit the floor hard, his body jerking and spasming; the volts ripped through his muscles and nerves. He was completely immobilized. Through his half-closed eyes he could see Xander and the rest of Strike Force looking at him like he was a circus act gone wrong.

Roll up, roll up to see the amazing electrocuted boy.

Xander whispered something to his teammates, watching Pete's agony with his deep brown eyes. The video kid had his camera in his hands, surreptitiously filming it all.

Pete had wanted to be the hero whose daring bravery would give the others a window to attack. He realized now, as he endured the shock buffeting his body, that he'd been nothing more than a guinea pig. The YouTuber had wanted to see what would happen before he chanced an escape attempt himself.

Xander had used him.

The betrayal hurt Pete even more than the shock. He felt the shackle finally switch off and he lay on his back on the cool concrete of the rooftop, groaning and staring up at the dropship above. Dwarfed beneath its wingspan, he felt small and foolish. Casey wouldn't have been this stupid. She would have seen through Xander's plan straight away.

Across the roof, the Red Eye grunts stepped forwards and reasserted their authority over the gamers, shoving them back into line. A couple of them noticed the video kid and advanced on him.

"Wait," said the boy, nervously putting down his camera. "It's nothing. I was just shooting some footage."

At the word *shooting* the Red Eyes raised their plasma rifles threateningly.

"No!" yelled the teenager. "Not that kind of shooting. I only shoot video." He sensed they didn't understand him. "Film – cinema. The magic of the moving image..."

One of the Red Eyes grabbed for the camera. The video kid dodged his grasp.

"Just give it to him," Xander growled at his teammate. "We don't need it. We've all seen what the necklaces do now."

"This footage is worth a fortune," the video kid said, cradling his camera protectively. "Imagine how many hits it'll get on YouTube. We could make millions."

"Don't be stupid," Xander hissed. "You're going to get yourself killed."

In a quick movement, one of the grunts knocked the camera out of the boy's hands, then stomped on it with his heavy black boot.

The other Red Eye grabbed his collar and hauled him into the air. He held the struggling boy up for all the gamers on the roof to see, turning around in a slow circle, like a magician holding a rabbit aloft before he makes it disappear.

"Klecht nan pardu," he told the gamers.

Pete guessed what he meant: *This is what happens if you try and fight back.*

"Don't," squealed the video kid. "Please…"

Before the boy could finish his sentence, the Red Eye threw him over the edge of the roof.

There was no scream. No sound at all, in fact.

The boy was there one second, then gone the next. There was a collective gasp from the gamers.

Somewhere in the queue someone started to whimper.

The overseer held the clicker over his head as if he was about to press it again. Terrified, the gamers fell back into line. Quite a few were sobbing now, the fear and tension of the day's events catching up with them. The shackles around their necks suddenly felt heavier than ever before. Even Xander looked pale, his easy confidence melting away as he kept his head down.

Pete, still stunned, felt himself being hauled onto his feet. He half expected to be the next person thrown off the rooftop, but he was shoved to the back of the line instead. He turned to stare questioningly at the overseer. In answer, the alien held up a black gloved hand and slowly counted on his fingers: *one … two … three … four …*

Then he pointed at Pete and added one more finger: *five.*

Pete realized what it meant. He was now the fifth member of Xander's squad, the replacement for the video kid. The lasers scanned the COMPETITOR badge around his neck. Casey's badge. There was a beep as he was accepted. The Red Eyes at the bottom of the ramp waved him on.

As Pete moved up the ramp into the belly of the alien spaceship, he took one last look at the rooftop behind him, taking in London's familiar skyline. He wasn't sure if he would ever see it again. He peered over the edge of the building and saw another rooftop below this one, a lower level that jutted out from the side of the building. In the centre was a swimming pool edged by sun loungers. The afternoon sunlight flickered over the blue water as it lapped back and forth, recently disturbed. Floundering in the middle of it, stunned from his fall but still alive, was the video kid.

The pool wasn't a myth after all.

17

BIG SISTER IS WATCHING YOU

Climbing the ladder in the lift shaft took less than five minutes but felt like days. Halfway up, the Ghost Reapers discovered the air vent that Cheeze had told them about. Casey yanked the grille off and they clambered inside. The vent was long and square, constructed from some kind of thin metal that buckled and popped under their combined weight. They made slow progress crawling along on their hands and knees. All the time Elite muttered under his breath, praying for it to be over.

Eventually, Casey spotted light at the end of the tunnel and saw a familiar face. "Fish!"

"They're coming!" the boy yelled over his shoulder to someone behind him. "This way, you guys."

Casey crawled out of the vent first, followed by the other two. Dropping into the shadows, they found themselves in a dimly lit room. The focal point of the room was a bank of monitors against the far wall. They showed images from dozens of surveillance cameras dotted around the shopping centre. In front of the monitors, bathed in their light, sat Cheeze. He spun around to greet them.

"You made it!" He grinned, rocking back and forth on his wheels in a little victory dance.

"What is this place?" Casey asked, staring around the room.

"It's like the nerve centre of the whole shopping centre," Cheeze explained, waving a hand around. "All the CCTV cameras, the public address system, environmental controls…"

"And the lifts, too," Fish butted in, eager not to let him hog the limelight. "That's how we rescued you. We stopped the lift before the Red Eyes got you."

"How?" Casey asked.

"I hacked into it," Cheeze said, pointing to the security console. He had unscrewed part of its casing and pulled out a bunch of wires as if he was hotwiring a car. His laptop sat near by, connected to the desk's circuit by a cable.

"Thank you," Casey said to Cheeze. "You saved our lives."

He reddened slightly.

Fish stared at them, irritated. He screwed up an empty sandwich packet and tossed it into the bin.

"Anyone got any scran?" he demanded, interrupting them. "I'm starving. My blood sugar's dropping like a stone."

Elite, who'd spent the last few minutes bent over with his hands on his knees, catching his breath after the ordeal of the vent, pulled a packet of Tic Tacs out of his pocket.

Fish grabbed them. "What flavour you got?"

"Strawberry."

"Ugh, they're the worst," he complained, then poured the entire pack into his mouth in one go. He tossed the empty plastic box back to Elite. "Thanks, though," he grunted, crunching the pink sweets noisily between his teeth. "You're a lifesaver."

"They were to share," Elite protested.

Cheeze spotted the plasma rifle on Casey's shoulder. He whistled, impressed.

"I got into a fight with a Red Eye in Starbucks," Casey explained.

"We saw you," Cheeze said, gesturing to the console. "You were amazing. How did you do all that?"

"I don't know," Casey mumbled, remembering the

way she had seemed to operate on pure instinct. "It just kind of happened."

"*Pfft.* I don't see why she's so amazing," said Fish. "I could have done that too if I'd had a gun like that."

Casey ignored him, her eyes flitting to the security desk. "You said you saw me? Where? On the screens?"

Cheeze nodded. "They have cameras all over the place. Must be a hundred at least."

"Maybe we can use them to find Pete," she said, her voice suddenly hopeful. She darted over to the security desk and stared at the controls. It was like the cockpit of a fighter jet. There were rows and rows of different-coloured buttons, a couple of joysticks and lots of switches.

"How do I use it?" she asked, impatient.

"You don't," Cheeze said, wheeling over and nudging her gently aside. "This is *my* toy." He cracked his knuckles with a flourish and turned to face her. "Just tell me where you want to look."

For the next ten minutes, Cheeze cycled through the various live feeds from the building's cameras. His hands ran over the camera controls like he was a concert pianist at a baby grand.

Casey stared at each new camera feed as it popped up on the monitors. But there was no sign of her brother. In fact, there was no sign of any of the gamers. "He's not here," she finally said, despondent. "It doesn't make any sense. Why can't we see him?" She felt her legs go weak. She didn't know how much longer she could go on.

"That guy Lee said the Red Eyes were rounding up the gamers," Brain said, remembering their earlier conversation.

"One of the shoppers told me the same thing," Casey whispered. "She said they were taking them up upstairs."

"So where are they?" Cheeze asked, flicking through the screens. Inside the stores they could see plenty of shoppers still cowering in fear, but no sign of any of the gamers from the tournament.

Casey's eyes began to ache from staring so hard at the grainy security camera footage.

"It doesn't make any sense," Brain mused. "We've been through every floor. They can't have just vanished into thin air."

"Thin air," Casey repeated, her mind whirring. "Thin air... Oh my God, the dropship!"

"What are you on about?" Fish said.

"The roof!" Casey said. "Show me the roof."

"I don't even know if there's a camera up there,"

Cheeze said as he cycled through the different feeds. He squinted at the control console until his eyes fell on a switch marked EXTERNAL FEEDS. He flipped it.

Casey and the boys gasped as they saw the lines of captured gamers being herded across the roof towards the dropship ramp.

"Look at the size of that thing!" Fish whistled. Brain and Elite pushed forwards, eager to get a better view of a vehicle they'd only ever seen in the game. As Casey searched the monitor screen, she saw Xander and the rest of Strike Force. Then, behind them, she finally spotted the face she'd been looking for.

"There he is! That's my brother."

Pete was heading up the dropship ramp. He looked pale and small. The Red Eyes towered over him. Cheeze grabbed a joystick on the console and zoomed in until the boy's anxious face filled the whole screen. Casey touched his cheek gently with her fingers. A second later, he disappeared inside the dropship and vanished from sight.

"Why aren't they taking any of the staff or the shoppers?" Cheeze asked. "Why do they only want gamers?"

Brain cleared his throat. "I have a theory,"

he announced. Everyone turned to look at him expectantly. "I think they're recruiting us."

Elite snorted in disbelief. "Recruiting us for what? *SkyWake*'s a game about a made-up war on a made-up planet. Unless London's about to be invaded by Squids, we ain't no use to nobody."

"Who says Hosin is made up?" Brain asked, speaking calmly and deliberately. He had clearly been chewing this over in his head for a while. "Before today, we all thought Red Eyes weren't real. But now here they are, with guns that work exactly like the ones in the game, taking the best players prisoner. I think they've been using the game to train us. That's why Casey knew how to use the plasma rifle."

"Sometimes we play as Squids, not Red Eyes," Cheeze pointed out, disbelieving.

"Best way to know your enemy…"

Elite shook his head. "This is mad, innit?"

"Maybe it's not," Casey said. "My dad told me that the military's been using games to train soldiers for years. Games teach you how to strategize, how to give and take orders, how to work together as a unit. *SkyWake* could be like a virtual training simulator."

"So what about Area 51?" Fish asked behind them. "Are you saying they're working with the aliens?"

"Maybe Area 51 *are* the aliens," Casey said, warming to the theory. "That brand management guy never met anyone from the company. He told us they did everything by email."

"But the Red Eyes can't even speak English," Cheeze pointed out. "There's no way they could have made a video game like *SkyWake*."

"Someone must be helping them." Brain shrugged. "Who?"

"How should I know? Someone who knows about video games, I guess."

The boys looked at one another uncertainly.

"Rubbish!" Fish said. "There's no way a bunch of aliens made a video game." He crossed his arms over his chest as if that settled the matter. But, as he did, he stared down at his *SkyWake* T-shirt nervously. He looked like he was regretting wearing something that pegged him as a *SkyWaker*.

"So what do we do now?" Cheeze asked.

There was a clatter as Casey reloaded her rifle. The gun's barrel opened up like the petals of a flower and released a belch of green plasma gas that smelled of bitter almonds. Then it closed again with a satisfied click. It was reloaded and ready to go. Just like her.

"I'm going to get my brother back."

"You can't, Casey," Cheeze warned. "It's suicide. Brain, tell her…"

"The probability of surviving against that many Red Eyes is less than zero," Brain said. "Even with that plasma rifle."

Elite sucked his teeth noisily. "It's all probability and logic with you, brainiac. This ain't a maths problem. Where's your heart?" He turned to Casey. "You go out there, girl, you're gonna get mashed up."

"Well, someone's got to do something," Casey said, standing tall with the plasma rifle in her hand. "What do you think will happen when all the gamers are onboard the dropship?" She mimed the ship blasting off with her free hand. "Those gamers need our help. Not just my brother – all of them."

"I'm not going anywhere," Fish said, shaking his head petulantly. "I'm staying put – right here, right where it's safe – and waiting to get rescued." He jabbed a finger at Casey and looked at the other boys for back-up. "All she's done today is get us into trouble. Girls are all the same, always ruining everything with their drama."

"Why do you have to be so toxic?" Cheeze demanded. "Shield tanks are supposed to protect their teams but all you do is have a go at everyone. It's not her fault your mum left."

"Guys, this isn't helping," Brain said sharply.

Fish put his hands on the sides of Cheeze's wheelchair, getting right in his face until they were almost nose to nose. He was furious at the mention of his mum.

"Don't touch my chair," Cheeze warned him, although Casey could tell he knew he'd overstepped the mark.

Fish ignored him. "If we go out there, she's gonna get us killed!" he shouted. "I don't care how much *SkyWake* we've played together, she's not a leader and we're not soldiers. Maybe if you weren't so lovesick, you'd be able to see that yourself."

"Wh-what are you on about?" Cheeze stammered.

"I've seen how you look at her," Fish continued gleefully, realizing he'd hit a nerve. "Oh Casey, you were *a-ma-zing*..."

Cheeze pushed Fish's hands off his wheelchair and spun away. His face burned red with embarrassment.

"Guys!" Brain said again, more insistent this time. "Someone's coming."

On the screens, a squad of human soldiers could be seen advancing through the underground car park beneath the shopping centre. They wore biohazard suits and carried automatic rifles. The leader approached a CCTV camera and peered into it until his face filled one of the monitors.

"This is Lieutenant Richard Dreyfus. Can anyone hear me?"

18

ALL YOUR BASE ARE BELONG TO US

Casey gasped as she saw Dreyfus's weather-beaten face up close.

"I know him. He was outside when I got here this morning. I spilled coffee over him."

"Well, he's inside now," Cheeze said. "That's the camera in the underground car park."

"How did they get in?" Casey asked.

"I heard this place was built over the Central Line," Brain said. "Maybe they found a way to get under the force field through the Tube tunnels."

"Sneaky," Fish whistled, impressed. "I bet those dozy Red Eyes don't even know what a Tube train is."

"If he can get in, it means we can get out," Brain continued, one step ahead of everyone as usual. The Ghost Reapers exchanged excited glances.

"Hello? Can anyone hear me?" Lieutenant Dreyfus's

voice was slightly out of sync with the movement of his lips on the CCTV monitor. It made him seem unnatural, as if he was contacting them from another dimension.

"We can hear you, Lieutenant," Casey said hurriedly into the microphone on the console. "We can see you too. You're on our screen in the security control room."

"We're coming to evacuate the building," Dreyfus told them. He clearly wasn't the kind of man to bother with pleasantries or introductions. "But first I need you to open up the security gates down here. They're locked tight."

Casey looked at Cheeze. He nodded, his fingers already reaching for the buttons.

"We're on it, Lieutenant," Casey said into the mic.

Dreyfus lifted a gloved hand into the air, giving the camera a thumbs-up.

"It's the cavalry," Fish said, bursting with relief. "I told you someone would come. These guys are the professionals. They're gonna get us out of here." He high-fived Elite and Brain. When he got to Casey, he let his hand drop sheepishly. "I'm sure they'll help you get your brother back, too," he mumbled, embarrassed.

"Thanks, Fish." Casey hoped he was right.

For the next half an hour, the soldiers secured the lower floors of the building. They worked quickly and professionally, ferrying the staff and shoppers to the underground car park. Casey, watching events unfold on the monitors, felt a warm tingle of relief. Maybe it *was* going to be OK. The soldiers would rescue Pete and this would all seem like a bad dream.

"Hey, where are all the Red Eyes?" Elite asked, noticing their absence. "They just chilling or what?"

"They're running scared," Fish sneered. "They know these soldier dudes are gonna go all *Call of Duty* on their alien butts."

Cheeze tapped the buttons on the console and brought up the camera feeds from the top floor. A dozen Red Eyes had taken up positions behind clam-shell-shaped energy shields at the top of the escalators outside the multiplex cinema. A couple of them carried supply crates full of weapons and ammo familiar from the game.

"They don't look very scared to me," he muttered, unwilling to start another argument with Fish. "It looks like they know the soldiers are coming in."

"That's a rearguard action," Brain said authoritatively, pushing his glasses up his nose. "It's what armies do when they retreat. They leave some troops behind to cover their backsides."

"The dropship must be getting ready to leave, then," Casey said, biting her lip. She thought of Pete being held prisoner inside. Who knew what the aliens might be doing to him in there? She remembered what Fish said about alien experiments and shuddered. Then she thought about Brain's theory that the Red Eyes were taking the gamers to fight on another planet. She wasn't sure what was worse. She only knew that she had to save her brother somehow.

Behind them, the doors to the control room burst open. Lieutenant Dreyfus stepped carefully through the narrow doorway, making sure not to snag his blue biohazard suit as he entered. Judging by the air tank on his back, the suit was designed to protect him from airborne toxins and diseases. The authorities were clearly taking no chances. He gently placed a chunky yellow box on the table, keeping it within easy reach.

"Where are the security guards?" he demanded, looking around for a responsible adult.

"It's just us," Cheeze told him. "We opened the gates for you."

If Dreyfus was impressed by their resourcefulness, he didn't show it.

"My men are evacuating everyone through the

tunnels beneath the building," he growled in his clipped, no-nonsense voice. "We have a decontamination tent set up outside beyond the force field. Once the building is clear, we'll nip this invasion in the bud."

"This isn't an invasion," Casey corrected him, stepping forwards. "They're abducting the gamers from the tournament."

A flicker of recognition passed over Dreyfus's face. He looked her up and down quickly, taking in her bubblegum-blue streaks, the military dog tags around her neck and, finally, the alien plasma rifle in her hands. His scowl deepened.

"Where did you get that?"

"I took it off one of the Red Eyes."

"Red Eyes?" the Lieutenant repeated, his eyebrows arching upwards in disbelief.

"It's what we call them in *SkyWake*." Casey could tell that the soldier didn't have a clue what she was talking about.

He took a step towards her and held out his hand. His baggy suit flapped around him like a balloon as the air inside redistributed.

"You need to give that to me, young lady. It's not a toy."

Casey instinctively gripped the gun a little tighter.

She didn't like this man.

"Not until you tell me how you're going to rescue the gamers. They took them to the dropship. My little brother's up there with them."

Dreyfus's brow furrowed behind his suit's Perspex visor. "That's not possible," he said, talking more to himself than the Ghost Reapers. "They've never abducted civilians before. It's not how they operate."

Casey felt her body tense up as she realized what he was saying. "You knew they were here, didn't you?" she said sharply, her face flushing with anger. "That's why you were waiting outside in the car park this morning. Why didn't you warn anyone?"

From upstairs, the sound of plasma rifles could be heard, followed by the *snap*, *crackle* and *pop* of automatic rifles.

"Give me a sit-rep," Dreyfus growled into his suit's microphone.

"We're encountering heavy resistance on the eighth floor, sir," said a soldier over the radio. "Multiple X-rays."

On the monitors, Casey saw that a firefight had erupted between the Red Eyes and the soldiers. Even though the footage was in grainy black and white, the battle looked intense. Dreyfus's men had run smack bang into the Red Eyes' rear-guard on the top floor of the building and the aliens were making short work of them. As the team watched, a Red Eye advanced towards the soldiers, his energy shield absorbing their bullets like a sponge.

"Look, that guy's a shield tank just like me," Fish exclaimed. He turned to Dreyfus eagerly. "There's no way your guys will be able to get through that energy shield. Not with ordinary bullets. Tell them to roll some grenades under it."

"My troops know what they're doing," Dreyfus said gruffly, although he was clearly disconcerted by the depth of Fish's knowledge of alien weaponry.

Brain studied the Red Eyes' advance. "They're like a *SkyWake* squad," he said. It was true. Each team of Red Eyes was comprised of five soldiers – assault, tank, sniper, medic and hacker – exactly like in the game.

"What is this *SkyWake* thing you keep talking about?" Dreyfus barked. "I've been seeing posters with its logo everywhere today."

Casey could see a thin film of sweat appearing on his brow inside the biohazard suit. She looked at the boys, but none of them wanted to be the one to explain it. It was clearly down to her.

She had to convince this soldier what was happening. He was her only hope of saving Pete. She took a deep breath.

"*SkyWake* is a video game. It's got guns exactly like this one and aliens just like the ones upstairs. We came here to play in the game's first ever global tournament. But halfway through, the Red Eyes sealed off the shopping centre and started abducting the players. We think they're recruiting us to fight for them." Dreyfus eyeballed the boys one by one. They all nodded nervously, confirming Casey's wild story.

Instead of belittling her theory, as Casey expected, Dreyfus was silent for a moment as he mulled it over. Then his weathered face clouded.

"You said it was a global tournament?"

"That's right." Brain nodded. "It's happening in six different cities around the world: London, New York… Oh no." His voice petered out as he realized what he was saying.

Thinking he'd simply forgotten the rest of the list, Fish picked up where Brain left off. "Plus Madrid, Johannesburg, Seoul and Dubai. They're running tournaments in shopping centres like this one all over the world." Fish paused, seeing the look of panic spreading over everyone's faces. "What did I say… ?"

Dreyfus growled into his radio. "Command, this

is Gold Leader. I need a sit-rep on extra-terrestrial activity in the following cities: New York, Madrid, Jo'burg, Seoul, Dubai. Same pattern of activity as London, including venue type."

"Stand by for update, Gold Leader."

"What's happening?" Fish asked. "I don't get it."

"All your base are belong to us," Brain muttered.

"What's that supposed to mean?" Fish demanded. "It's not even proper English." He clearly didn't share Brain's knowledge of old memes.

"It means they're not just abducting people in London," Casey told Fish. "They're doing it in all those other cities, too. They must be building an army of gamers from all around the world." She turned to Dreyfus, imploring him to help. "You have to rescue my brother before that ship leaves."

Before Dreyfus could respond, his radio crackled again.

"Lieutenant, this is Tucker. We've captured a live one."

19

I'M NOT A COWARD, I'M JUST OVERLY PERCEPTIVE OF RISK

Pete's dad used to say his son wanted to run before he could walk. It had always annoyed Pete … mostly because it was true. He was always impatient to be more grown up than he actually was, and it often got him into trouble. He thought about this as he shuffled through the dropship's corridors with the other miserable gamers. He wished, now more than ever, that he'd stayed with Casey. She would have kept him safe.

The Red Eyes were escorting the gamers into the belly of the dropship towards the loadout bay. As the huge blast doors slid open to admit them, Pete already knew what to expect. In *SkyWake* the loadout bay was where Red Eye soldiers prepped for battle, where they were kitted out with armour and weapons by huge mechanical arms that swung around in the gloom like assembly-line robots in a car factory.

Ahead of them was a moving walkway that ran like a conveyor belt between banks of machinery, slowly propelling the gamers along its length in single file until they vanished into the gloom beyond. A cacophony of industrial noise echoed all around and the air was thick with the stench of grease and hydraulic fluid.

As Pete was shoved onto the walkway, bringing up the rear behind Strike Force and the other captured gamers, he cursed his stupidity. He'd let himself get shocked just so that Xander could see what would happen – and it had all been for nothing.

The YouTuber must have felt Pete's eyes drilling into the back of his skull because he turned around to face him and mumbled something indistinct.

"What was that?" Pete asked warily.

"I said, you showed a lot of heart back there," Xander repeated. He tugged at his Strike Force eSports jersey, with its logo of a fist clutching a bloody heart, as if to make his point. Then he added, "How you holding up?"

Despite himself, Pete was secretly pleased by Xander's concern. "I'm OK," he said, even though he was feeling anything but. His body still hadn't fully recovered from the shock he'd received, and he felt giddy and sick. "I'm tougher than I look."

Xander sucked his teeth and nodded appreciatively. "They really fried you," he said, tugging at the shackle around his own neck. "What do you think it was? Some kind of electrical current?"

"Possibly." Pete shrugged. "I got a shock off a light switch once. It was like that, only stronger."

"Do you know what conduction is?" Xander asked, one eye on the Red Eyes standing guard along the sides of the moving walkway.

"You mean how electricity flows through metal or water?" Pete said, thinking back to the experiments he'd done in science. They'd tried running an electrical current through metal, wood and even a banana.

Xander nodded. "What do you think would happen if you were touching a Red Eye when you got zapped?" he asked. "Would the shock be conducted by their power armour?"

Pete considered the question. It was as if he'd suddenly become the world authority on alien shock technology. He quite liked it.

"I think it would," he said after a pause. It was really nothing more than a guess. Then, worrying where Xander might be going with this, he quickly added, "but I'm not gonna be your guinea pig again."

The YouTuber nodded. "Fair enough. You've done your bit. And you did it better than any of these losers would have done." He gestured towards the rest of Strike Force just ahead of him. "They've all bottled it."

It was true. Xander's teammates looked utterly broken. Seeing Pete get electrocuted and then the video kid being thrown off the building had crushed them.

Xander glanced around the loadout bay thoughtfully. "This is probably our last chance to get out of here," he told Pete. "The guards are pretty spread out."

"You'll never free everyone."

"Oh, it's too late for that," Xander scoffed, as if amused by Pete's idealism. "I'm just trying to save my own skin. Someone's got to escape. It might as well be us."

Pete gulped, realizing the implications of what Xander was saying. They were going to abandon everyone. He wasn't sure how he felt about that.

"Maybe we should wait a little longer," he suggested. "We might be able to—"

"You haven't been paying attention," Xander told him. "Look at the helmets."

Pete followed Xander's gaze. The last stage in the

production line, after each gamer had been fitted with armour and weapons, was something Pete had never seen in the game. He watched as a robotic arm placed a wire mesh cap, like a hairnet, over each gamer's head.

The minute the cap was in place, sharp prongs jabbed into the gamer's temples, drawing beads of blood, and the mesh lit up in a flicker of LED lights. At the same moment, another robot arm swung past and fitted a combat helmet over the top. Then, with a vicious twist, it removed the neck shackles.

Pete wondered why the gamers didn't run the moment they were free. It took him a moment to notice the difference. As soon as they were fitted with the mesh, the gamers' posture changed. They suddenly stood up straight, their bodies rigid, their eyes blank and glassy.

"It's some kind of mind-control device," Xander explained. Pete's jaw was slack with fear. He didn't think it was possible to feel more terrified. That was going to be their fate too, in just a few minutes.

"Before we get to the end of the walkway, I'm going to take out that overseer," Xander said, nodding up ahead. "I need you to grab his energy sword. Can you do that?"

Pete looked up. Xander was right. There was only one Red Eye near by now, the overseer with the clicker. This really was their last chance to get off the ship before they were taken who knew where.

"I'll take the shock this time," Xander promised. "I need you to make the most of the opportunity. I can't do this without you. Grab his energy sword, take him out and then help me back on my feet."

Pete could hear the desperation in Xander's voice. It was just the two of them now. Him and the famous YouTuber. They'd be comrades-in-arms. He imagined Xander telling his million plus subscribers about how they'd survived this moment together.

"I'm in," Pete said.

Xander grunted, relieved.

But before Xander could say anything more, a robotic arm swung towards him and cut away his trainers with a laser beam. Another arm then swung in and replaced them with combat boots that fitted around his ankles in sections and gelled together. A second later, the same thing happened to Pete. He looked down as the boots fitted tightly around his ankles. There was a whirr above him and an armoured chest plate descended, held by two robotic arms.

The armour came over Pete's head, causing him to

panic momentarily as his vision turned black. Then it hissed and clicked across his sternum as it locked into position. Metal rods shot out and connected it to the other pieces of armour that were slowly being placed on his arms and legs.

Looking down at his new outfit, he saw it was an exo-suit, a series of interconnected rods and armoured plates. It wasn't as fancy as the Red Eyes' power armour, but it would protect and strengthen his body when it was activated.

"See you on the other side, kid," Xander whispered, pushing his fringe out of his eyes so he could get a better view of the robot arm carrying the strange mesh net that was swinging towards him.

The words were barely out of his mouth before he leaped into action, ducking under the mesh net and launching himself off the walkway towards the nearby overseer. The alien, seeing him coming, reached for his clicker. Xander crashed into him, wrapping his arms and legs around the Red Eye just as the overseer hit the button.

Xander's body jerked and stuttered as the shock shackle burst into life. He clung on to the overseer's armoured chest with every ounce of strength in his body, refusing to let go.

For a moment, Pete thought they'd made a mistake. Maybe whatever alien materials the Red Eyes' suits were made of didn't conduct electricity. But then the overseer started to convulse as the volts from Xander's body zapped into his armoured chest. Xander held on for dear life, like he was riding a bucking bronco.

With a hiss of black smoke, the alien's suit finally seized up and they both toppled to the ground. The overseer's energy sword fell off his belt and rolled across the ground towards Pete's feet.

Pete stared at it.

This was his moment.

All he had to do was bend down and pick it up.

He didn't move.

"Grab ... it ... kid!" Xander hissed through clenched teeth as the last of the volts from his shock shackle ran through his body. "Take ... him ... out!"

Pete imagined picking up the sword and skewering the overseer before fighting his way off the dropship with Xander.

He'd be a hero.

He tried to step forward, but his legs wouldn't move. They were rigid with fear. He saw the hope dying in Xander's eyes. As it waned, it was replaced with something else. A look of utter contempt.

There was a shout along the walkway. The Red Eye grunts had seen the scuffle and were hurrying towards them. Pete looked at the sword handle again. Picking it up would mean he'd made a choice. A choice to stay and fight and, perhaps, even to die.

His legs started to move. He took one step and then another and, before he even knew what was happening, he was breaking into a sprint. But he wasn't running towards the sword. He was running away from it, back along the walkway.

"Stop…" Xander pleaded weakly as Pete fled.

But Pete didn't stop.

He couldn't stop.

He had only one thought in his head.

Hide.

20

WE COME IN PEACE,
SHOOT TO KILL

Casey recognized the captured Red Eye the moment he was wheeled into the security control room. It was the one she'd named Scratch. He was lying on a gurney, one of those medical stretchers on wheels that paramedics use, steered by two soldiers in biohazard suits. They were the man and woman she'd spotted in the back of the minivan that morning.

The man's name patch read TUCKER. He was young and eager and carried an assault rifle and backpack. The woman's patch read WILSON. She had short hair and a pinched, serious face. She carried a bulky medical bag with a big red cross on it.

"We found it in a coffee shop downstairs," Tucker told Dreyfus. He was out of breath. The bulky biohazard suits made moving around difficult.

"He's the one who chased me," Casey said. Seeing

Scratch's battered armour, she suddenly felt guilty that her first interaction with a visitor from another planet had been to blow it up. "I didn't mean to kill him," she added.

"You didn't," Wilson said, pushing her aside. "You just busted its suit."

"Open it up," Dreyfus commanded. "I want to see it."

With Tucker's help, Wilson heaved Scratch off the gurney and onto the table. It was just long enough to hold him. Wilson ran a gloved hand over the alien's power armour, feeling its contours. From somewhere upstairs came the muffled sound of gunfire as the rest of the soldiers fought the aliens on the upper floors.

"We don't have time for this," Casey said, impatient. "My brother—"

"We can spare a minute or two," Dreyfus interrupted. "Maybe this thing can tell us exactly what's going on."

Tucker pulled a laptop from his backpack and flipped it open. On the screen was some kind of translation software. A list of Arcturian glyphs sat side by side with a selection of English words.

"Woah, sweet app," Cheeze said, wheeling himself

over to take a closer look. "You know how to speak their language?"

Tucker turned the screen away from him. "It's classified," he warned. "Stay back."

"You've met these things before, haven't you?" Casey whispered, looking at Dreyfus. Her eyes fell on the purple patch on his neck. She realized it wasn't a birth mark or a scar. It looked like a plasma burn.

"First contact was a decade ago," Dreyfus told her, his voice bitter. "My squad was on patrol in Iraq when they ambushed us. They killed my men, abducted my radio operator. I was the only survivor. I've been tracking them ever since."

"Why would they abduct soldiers?" Fish asked.

"Like I told you," Brain said, exasperated, "they're trying to build an army. Don't you see? It's—"

A piercing shriek made everyone jump. Wilson was cutting through the alien's power suit with a handheld angle grinder. The circular blade threw out sparks as it sliced into the strange metal.

"It's thicker than a rhino's arse!" Tucker shouted over the noise. He was like a big kid. A burning smell floated across the room, filling the team's nostrils and making them choke. The soldiers, encased in their airtight biohazard suits, didn't notice it.

Dreyfus's radio crackled.

"Gold Leader, I have your update. Over," said a voice. "We're receiving multiple reports of extra-terrestrial activity. Madrid and Johannesburg have issued alerts in the last few minutes. We're still trying to establish contact with Dubai, Seoul and New York. They've gone dark."

"It has to be an invasion," Tucker said. He sounded scared and excited at the same time, like someone on a roller coaster. "Finally, we'll get to have a stand-up fight with these things."

"I already told you, they're not invading us to take over the planet," Casey said impatiently. "They've come to kidnap gamers. You have to go up there and stop them."

Dreyfus looked at her with a frown. His eyes moved to Scratch. "Let's ask it," he said decisively. He turned to Wilson. "Are you ready, Sergeant?"

"Almost," Wilson replied, putting down the angle grinder. "Tucker, come and grab the other side. On my count. Three ... two ... one ... PULL!"

The two soldiers yanked the alien's thick black chest plate. It came away from the rest of the suit with a sucking sound.

Casey gasped as she saw the alien inside.

Scratch was about two metres tall with scaly orange skin that was wrinkled and saggy like an iguana's and eyes that were as black as obsidian.

"God, he's ugly," Tucker grimaced, turning away as if he might throw up inside his suit.

"It's not a 'he'," Wilson corrected him. "It's a female."

Casey, surprised, stared at the alien as she writhed on the table and the interlocking sections that made up her mouth revealed rows of vicious-looking teeth. The alien groaned and covered her eyes with her talon-like hands. The light was hurting her.

Wilson examined the interior of the suit. It was coated in a black gloop that clung to the metal casing. Electrodes ran from Scratch's head and spine into the suit's circuitry. Scratch struggled as Wilson poked around.

"You're hurting her," Casey said. Without her power armour Scratch looked helpless and defenceless.

Dreyfus leaned over Scratch until his Perspex visor was right in her face. If it wasn't for the plastic between them, their foreheads would have touched. Casey could feel his burning desire for revenge. It prickled in the air around him like an invisible aura. She wondered what exactly had happened to him out in Iraq all those years ago.

"I've waited for this moment a long time," he whispered to the alien as it lay on its back. "What do you have to say to me?"

"Icht hafu ran gestar. Wecht na rechtu?" the laptop said, translating Dreyfus's words into the strange guttural language that the Red Eyes used.

Scratch stared at the laptop suspiciously, surprised to hear her native tongue. *"Icht tenlach hef hominide,"* she hissed, returning her steely gaze to Dreyfus. Her eyelids blinked sideways like a lizard's. The effect was unnerving. There was a second or two of lag as the computer turned her words into English.

"I see you, human," the laptop said in a jerky, digital voice that lacked intonation. It made Casey shudder.

"And I see you, as you really are, without your armour," Dreyfus said, with a hint of mockery. He spoke slowly to let the software catch every word. "Tell me why you're here. What do you want from us?" He waited for the translation.

"Mecht granthan quesh hefna loa, imbeci," Scratch replied.

"Our goals are beyond your understanding, pathetic creature," the computer translated. The Ghost Reapers watched the alien in frozen horror, unable to avert their eyes. The way Scratch's strange mouth moved, each section flapping as she spoke, was chilling.

"How are you planning to invade us?" Dreyfus asked. The laptop translated. Scratch didn't answer.

Casey pushed forwards. She'd had enough of waiting around. If the lieutenant couldn't ask the right questions, she would.

"Why are you taking the gamers?" she demanded. "Why did you take my brother? Are you using them as soldiers? On Hosin?"

Scratch turned and looked at Casey as the app translated Casey's questions. Her eyes were so black, and so large, Casey could see herself reflected in them. She glanced down at the plasma rifle – *her* plasma rifle – in Casey's hands and her strange mouth twitched into an ugly sneer as she hissed her reply.

"You're the one who did this to me," came the translation. "On my planet, we would salute you for your bravery. If your brother is half as skilled as you, he will serve us well."

"No!!" Casey shouted, overcome with panic. "You can't take him!"

Dreyfus leaned over Scratch again. "We won't let you invade us," he said firmly. "We have troops and tanks and helicopters waiting outside the building to stop you."

The alien's eyes fell on the purple scar on Dreyfus's neck. "What kind of a planet is it where your children fight better than you do?" she asked with a sneer. "When the time comes, Arcturia will crush you just like we have crushed all those who stand in our way."

"Over my dead body," Dreyfus spat.

"Yes," Scratch agreed, "it most certainly will be."

A chill fell over the room.

Casey could see that Dreyfus was rattled.

"I've heard enough," he said. "Put this thing in the quarantine tent. We'll see what more it wants to say when we get it back to base."

Wilson pulled Scratch out of the armour, yanking the electrodes off her head and spine. The alien's body contorted and she made a noise like a strangled shriek. Everyone winced.

It was like being stabbed in the ears with a kitchen knife.

Wilson and Tucker lifted Scratch onto the gurney. They pulled a quarantine cover over the alien and zipped it shut. The alien stopped writhing but the shriek continued beneath the plastic. It was getting louder and louder.

"What's it doing?" Tucker asked, pale. "Is it trying to attack us?"

"No," Casey said, realizing the truth. "She's calling."

"Calling? Calling for what?" Dreyfus demanded.

"Help."

21

TARANTULAS

Scratch's piercing screech stopped as quickly as it had begun, and the alien slumped back onto the gurney.

"Is it dead?" Tucker asked.

"No, she's still breathing," said Wilson. "But if we want to keep her alive for questioning, we need to get her to the containment facility."

Dreyfus nodded. "Tell everyone to—"

There was a sudden screech of static on the soldiers' radios.

"Pull back! Pull back! We're being overrun!" a panicked voice yelled. At the same moment, there was a sudden burst of gunfire upstairs and then what sounded like an explosion.

"What's going on?" Dreyfus snapped, speaking into his radio.

"They're all over us, sir!" shouted a female voice.

It was hard to make out her words over the sound of plasma rifles blasting in the background. "We're on the top floor of the building. We can't—"

There was another burst of plasma fire and then a scream and then silence.

"Sergeant?" Dreyfus barked into the radio. "Can you hear me...?"

The Ghost Reapers watched the monitors in horror as the Red Eyes overwhelmed the soldiers. The aliens showed no mercy, firing left and right at the advancing humans and blasting them with plasma fire. The soldiers, outgunned and outnumbered, retreated downstairs, dragging their wounded comrades with them.

"They're wiping your guys out!" Fish shouted, shocked. "You have to do something."

Dreyfus stiffened and his eyes flitted to the chunky yellow box that he'd placed on the table when he first came into the control room.

"We have an insurance policy," he said.

"What kind of insurance policy?" Casey demanded.

"I bet they're going to blow the building," Brain said. It was just a hunch but, judging by the expression on Dreyfus's face, it was close to the truth.

"You can't!" Casey cried, her heart thumping

against her chest. "What about my brother? And the gamers?" Her hopes of rescuing Pete seemed to be slipping away right in front of her eyes.

"I won't let those things launch an attack on London," Dreyfus told her. His voice was horribly flat and final. "God knows how many of your *Red Eyes* are on that dropship on the roof. My orders are to protect the city."

Casey shook her head, her eyes filling with tears. "My dad was a soldier," she said. "He told me that being in charge means looking after people. Those gamers upstairs are your responsibility."

"Sometimes soldiers have to make difficult choices," Dreyfus said. "If your father was here, he'd understand."

Dreyfus moved to pick up the yellow box. Casey blocked his way. She hefted the plasma rifle onto her shoulder and pointed it at the lieutenant's chest.

"My dad's dead," she said, furious. "He got blown up by a car bomb outside a school in Afghanistan because a bunch of terrorists didn't think girls should be allowed to get an education. He died trying to save lives, not take them. He wouldn't have understood you at all."

Dreyfus raised one eyebrow at the alien weapon

pointing at him. "You don't have it in you," he said.

Casey knew he was right. She couldn't pull the trigger. Not like this. But if she didn't, how could she save Pete?

The lieutenant took a step towards her. A trickle of salty sweat ran down the bridge of Casey's nose. She wanted to wipe it away, but she didn't dare take her hands off the rifle.

There was a soft *click-clack*.

So quiet at first that it was barely noticeable.

Then another. And another.

It sounded like metal tapping metal. Casey looked up at the ceiling. The noise seemed to be getting faster and louder with each passing second, like a pair of castanets clicking.

"Something's coming," Casey whispered.

Dreyfus and the soldiers didn't look convinced, but the boys held their breath as they listened. They were getting used to trusting Casey's instincts.

"Up there," Brain said, looking at the air vent they'd climbed through earlier. Dreyfus drew a pistol from a pocket on his suit. The weapon looked strange in his rubber-gloved hand.

Casey pushed a chair against the wall under the vent and climbed onto it. She stuck her head through the opening and peered inside. The tapping was definitely coming from further along the vent, echoing down its metal walls.

"What is it?" Dreyfus asked behind her. "What's in there?"

Casey saw their shadows first. The black silhouettes flickered against the metal walls of the vent as they approached the final bend before the control room. She recognized the outline of their sleek bodies and their spindly metal legs.

"Tarantulas!!" she yelled, toppling backwards off her chair in panic as a dozen of the spider bots clattered along the vent towards her. Each robot was falling over the others in its haste to attack.

These were the reinforcements Scratch had called for – hunter killer robots designed to clear out small confined spaces. They swarmed into the room, scuttling across the walls, floor and ceiling as they advanced.

The soldiers, ignorant of *SkyWake*'s weaponry, stared in surprise as the metallic tarantulas leaped towards them, their bodies reflecting the glare of the CCTV monitors. Two spiders landed on the back of Tucker's biohazard suit and there was a hiss of escaping air as their sharp legs punctured the plastic.

He flailed, trying to knock them off.

Wilson ran to help him, but a third tarantula crawled across the floor and jumped onto her leg. It ripped through her biohazard suit, burrowing under the plastic folds. She screamed and flapped around helplessly as it crawled over her skin inside the suit. When it reached her neck, it bit into her flesh with its paralysing fangs and she slumped to the floor. Tucker collapsed next to her a moment later.

Dreyfus, seeing how close they were to being overrun, tried to grab the detonator box from the table. But Fish was too quick for him. He snatched it from the soldier's grasp and dived under the security desk with it.

Cursing, Dreyfus tried to pull him out but had to stop as the rest of the spider bots swarmed the room. He opened fire with his pistol. All his bullets went wide of their targets. The tarantulas' bodies were no bigger than pebbles you might find on a beach, and their long, thin legs enabled them to leap from floor to wall to ceiling faster than he could shoot.

Across the room, Casey and her friends were fighting their own battle. A spider bot landed on Cheeze's lap and jabbed at him with its pincers. Brain grabbed the bot from behind and threw it hard against the wall, smashing it to pieces.

Three more dropped from the ceiling and encircled Casey. She dodged left and right, trying to get past them, but they were too quick for her. They closed in, clicking menacingly, their pincers dripping with neurotoxin venom.

Instinctively, she jumped on the table and brought her plasma rifle up to her shoulder. She felt her perception of time slowing, as if she was caught in a slipstream where the seconds turned into minutes and the minutes became hours. It was happening again, the same feeling she'd had back in the coffee shop. Her mind tuned out, like a radio shifting from a station to white noise.

The rifle in her hands shot three times. She knew it was her finger on the trigger but she didn't even remember making the decision to fire. She hit her targets with deadly accuracy, blasting all three spiders as they jumped.

The boys looked on in awe. Standing there with her blue hair and the gun in her hand, she looked like some kind of ferocious battle angel from a manga comic.

More tarantulas burst through the vent. A couple landed on the gurney and scurried over the plastic tent, checking Scratch was still alive. Meanwhile, there was a series of heavy thumps on the door to the room as someone tried to break through. On the monitors, four alien grunts could be seen in the corridor outside, shoulders charging the door.

"We've got to get out of here!" Casey shouted to her teammates.

"But there's only one exit," Cheeze warned, his voice panicked. The Red Eyes would burst through the doors at any moment, the lock was too flimsy to hold them.

"We'll have to make another one then," Casey said. She jumped off the table and lifted her rifle to her shoulder. A blast of green plasma cut through the wall behind the boys, creating a makeshift exit through the bricks. Fish was the first to run towards it, holding the yellow box tight under his arm as he escaped between the seared and smoking brickwork.

"No!" Dreyfus yelled. "I need that detonator."

He raised his pistol. But he was swarmed by tarantulas before he could pull the trigger. He fell to the floor, the air inside his biohazard suit rippling around him as he tried to push off the bots. At the same moment the Red Eyes burst through the doors, plasma rifles blazing.

Casey ducked into the hole she'd created in the wall, using the smoking bricks as cover. She turned and laid down fire as the boys ran towards her to safety. Cheeze was the last to flee, frantically pumping the tyres of his wheelchair. He was halfway across the room when a tarantula pounced. It locked onto one of his wheels, toppling the chair over. He fell face first onto the floor.

More tarantulas swarmed over his wheelchair in a pack, tearing at it with their metal pincers as if they thought it was some kind of threat. Cheeze pulled himself free and clambered along the floor on his belly, dragging his legs behind him, desperate to escape.

"Cheeze!" Casey yelled, peering back into the room and firing over him at the Red Eyes across the room. Two blasts of return fire seared into the wall beside her. She ducked, cursing. When she looked back around the broken wall, she saw that the tarantulas had now completely destroyed the wheelchair and were in pursuit of Cheeze.

Casey raised her rifle to fire again. But the Red Eyes saw her and opened up on her position. She ducked back into cover, suppressed by enemy fire, as plasma bursts chewed through the wall.

She felt a hand pulling at her shoulder.

"Casey, we've got to move." It was Brain.

"But, Cheeze…!"

They both looked back around the broken brick-work. The Red Eyes had taken possession of the control room and were disarming Dreyfus. The remaining tarantulas were moving towards the hole in the wall, moving in a pack. They'd be on them in seconds.

"We have to go," Brain warned her again, trying to pull her away.

Casey shook him off, unwilling to give up. As she raised her rifle to fire, she locked eyes with Cheeze. There was no way she could save him. She could see the fear and despair in his face. He nodded, as if to tell her it wasn't her fault.

"Run!" he shouted. "Keep the others safe. I—"

His final words strangled in his throat as the tarantulas pounced onto his back. One nipped at his paralysed legs. It seemed surprised by his lack of reaction.

Another scurried up his spine towards his head, preparing to bite his neck.

Before Casey saw what happened next, Elite locked his arms around her waist and pulled her away, surprising her with his wiry strength. He bundled her along the corridor behind Brain and Fish.

Hot tears streaked her cheeks as she ran.

22

ENTER YOUR INITIALS

On the afternoon they buried Casey's dad, the house was full of mourners. There was the vicar from the church, several members of her dad's regiment, and various friends and family. Her mum wore a simple black dress. Casey thought she looked beautiful in a sad kind of way.

The news of her father's death had come ten days before. When Casey saw the two stony-faced casualty notification officers walk up the driveway, she had known her life was about to change for ever.

The soldiers said that Lieutenant Michael Henderson had been killed trying to defuse an improvised explosive device outside a school in Kabul in Afghanistan. *Device* was the word the soldiers used. It was as if they thought *bomb* was too ugly.

The guests came to the wake directly after the

service. They chatted and drank coffee and ate food from the buffet that Casey's aunts had laid out in the kitchen. Casey wanted to scream. She couldn't bear all these people being in her house. It felt so fake and wrong. Why was everyone chatting politely when all she wanted to do was yell and break things? How could the rest of the world keep on turning as if nothing had happened?

When no one was looking, she snuck out and headed into the garage. The arcade machine was waiting for her between the tool racks. She wiped away her tears and hung her dad's dog tags, the spare ones he kept in his bedside drawer, over the corner of the cabinet. No one had found the ones he'd worn when he was killed. She had expected to see him wearing them, lying in his coffin in his formal dress uniform just like in the movies. But, because of the power of the bomb, the coffin had been closed.

The arcade machine beeped at her as it booted up. She hadn't played it for weeks, not since the night her dad announced he was being deployed. The screen flashed, enticing her to begin. She placed her hands on the controls.

"What are you doing?" Pete asked angrily. He'd followed her into the garage and now stood behind her, his figure reflected in the cabinet's screen.

"Nothing."

"Mum told me to come and get you. She says you have to stay until all the guests are gone. It's rude."

Casey didn't turn around. "I'll be there in a minute."

Pete waited a moment, staring at her back as she stood in front of the machine. "I don't know why you like that stupid game."

"Dad didn't think it was stupid."

"Well, I do. You and him spent all summer playing it. I barely got to see him. And now he's gone. It's not fair."

"We asked you to join us," Casey said, turning around. "But you just wanted to play *Fortnite*. It was your choice."

"Shut up!" Pete yelled, furious. "Just shut up."

Casey shook her head at him. "Why are you always so immature?"

"Because I'm not perfect like you."

"Who says I'm perfect?" she asked, surprised.

"I do. *Look at me, I'm Casey, the perfect gamer. I'm Casey, the perfect daughter.* Well you know what you're not perfect at? Being my sister."

With that, he stormed out of the garage. Casey thought about going after him, but she didn't know what to say. He was angry and sad. She got that. But she was too. It wasn't fair of him to blame her for everything. Part of her did feel guilty, though. She'd enjoyed the time she'd had with her dad that summer and, if she was truthful, she'd liked not having Pete around to share it.

The machine bleeped, reminding her that it was waiting. She pressed the **1 PLAYER** button and watched the familiar rows of aliens appear. They advanced slowly across the screen as the game's throbbing bass pounded the speakers.

Duh-dah. Duh-dah. Duh-dah. Duh-dah. Duh-dah. Duh-dah. Duh-dah.

Casey started shooting right away. Her gun turret slid from left to right as she counted her shots in her head.

Move. Stop. Shoot.

Within a couple of minutes, she'd cleared the first wave, blasting through the rows and columns of their attack until there were none left. The game reset and the next wave advanced on her, faster than the last. She skidded her gun turret along the bottom of the screen again ... straight into a missile from a crab-shaped invader. Her gunship exploded.

She cursed. She now had two lives left.

For the next few minutes she worked methodically and slowly, blasting through screen after screen of invaders. Her hands darted over the controls. Her index finger ached from hammering the fire button.

Move. Stop ... "No!"

Her turret exploded as it was hit by another missile. Why hadn't she seen it coming? She stared at her score unhappily. It wasn't anywhere near her personal best, let alone her dad's high score. She took a deep breath and carried on. One life left.

She shot six invaders, then dodged a falling missile by sliding under the cover of one of her bases. That was close. Then she blasted through the base's defensive cover, creating a narrow channel through it that her turret could shoot up. A crab-shaped alien above her exploded into diagonal lines as she scored a direct hit. She resisted the urge to punch the air. She had to focus.

The mysterious UFO raced across the top of the screen, sirens blaring. She was ready for it and caught it with her twenty-third shot, just like her dad had taught her, to get bonus points.

Her score spun upwards. She didn't even look at it.

Move. Stop ...

Shoot.

Her mind emptied and she became totally immersed in the game. Nothing in the universe mattered except for this brave little gunship fighting to stop the relentless tide of advancing aliens. Her hands flew over the controls. Her fingers moved without needing to be told what to do.

Time slowed right down. She wasn't thinking about anything. She wasn't worrying about anything. She wasn't even mourning her dead dad any more.

She was in the zone.

This, *this* was flow.

She blasted through another set of aliens until only one remained. The final squid raced across the screen at supersonic speed, getting closer and closer to her gunship. If she didn't catch him, it was game over. She breathed in through her nose and out through her mouth. Her heartbeat matched the *duh-dah, duh-dah* of the game's sound. A feeling of immense calm came over her.

Move.

Stop.

Shoot!

The last invader exploded. Her high score hit 17,180.

And then, without ceremony, the screen reset

and five new rows of aliens began to descend on her gun turret. She realized that she could never win this game. It was relentless. The invaders never stopped.

It suddenly occurred to her that all along the only person she had been trying to beat was her dad. She was hit by a wave of sadness and took her hands off the controls. Her gun turret sat at the bottom of the screen, motionless. She watched as an invader's missile fell towards it and scored a direct hit. It exploded.

GAME OVER.

The machine asked her to enter her initials. She tapped the buttons, writing out a **K** and then a **C** and then an **H** to represent "Casey Henderson".

She looked at it. It didn't seem right. She chewed her lip and tapped the buttons again, changing the last letter.

It now read **KCF**. Casey Flow.

The high score table appeared. **KCF** was in first place. **MCH**, her dad, was now in second place. She didn't feel elated or even pleased, just a little empty inside.

She picked up the dog tags hanging over the edge of the cabinet and put them around her neck. The metal felt cold against her skin. Then she flipped the power switch on the wall and the picture on the screen imploded, shrinking down until it was a tiny white dot in the middle of the monitor. It blinked and vanished.

She never turned it on again.

23

DON'T BE A DUMMY,
YOU DUMMY

Casey sat perched on a display plinth in Next, surrounded by a family of mannequins wearing beach outfits. They looked happy and carefree, the exact opposite of how she felt. The plasma rifle lay at her feet. She didn't want to carry it any more. She didn't want to do anything any more. She'd had enough of running and fighting, enough of trying to fix what was impossible to fix. She held her head in her hands and closed her eyes.

She expected to hear the nagging voice in the back of her head telling her how rubbish she was. But it didn't come. Maybe it didn't need to. It had done its job and it had been right all along. She *was* a failure. She thought of Cheeze, and even Dreyfus and his soldiers, left to the mercy of the alien invaders. But, most of all, she thought of Pete on the dropship on the roof.

"It's all my fault," she whispered to herself. "I've lost everyone today." She felt her body heave as she let out the sobs she hadn't known she'd been holding back. Once she started crying, she wondered if she'd ever stop.

"Nobody could have done anything differently," Brain said quietly, sitting beside her. "Statistically, our chances—"

"Nobody cares about your statistics, bruv," Elite told him testily. "We lost Cheeze, and Casey lost her little brother. No amount of statistics or logic can explain how to feel about that."

"I know," Brain whispered, taking off his glasses and wiping his own eyes.

Elite stared at the floor, his gaze fixed on his scuffed white trainers. "I know you know, brainiac," he said, relenting. "It's not your fault. I feel you."

He gave Brain a fist bump.

"Quiet," Fish hissed from the shop doorway where he was on watch for Red Eyes. "Someone's coming."

The Ghost Reapers fell silent as they heard movement outside. Peering between the mannequins, the team saw the squad of Red Eyes that had attacked the security control room coming back up the escalators. Two of them were carrying the gurney with Scratch on it. The others guarded a prisoner.

It was Dreyfus.

The military man had been stripped of his biohazard suit. He looked naked without it, dressed in just cargo trousers and an olive-green polo shirt. He wore a heavy shackle around his neck. Casey could tell from his body language that he was furious about being captured. She waited, hoping to see Cheeze. But there was no sign of their teammate, nor the soldiers Wilson and Tucker.

After the aliens had safely passed, Fish returned to the group. He still held the yellow detonator box under his arm.

"What do we do now?" he asked

"We need to get downstairs and go out through the tunnel," Casey said.

"And then what?" Fish asked. "What if the people in charge outside want to blow the place up too? All day long you've been telling us how we need to rescue everyone."

"And all day long you've been telling me the truth," Casey replied. "You were right. I'm not a leader and we're not a crack military team. It was fun while we were playing in our bedrooms with our headsets on. But this is something else. It's over."

Elite sucked his teeth. "If we go downstairs now, it'll be like logging off in the middle of a game," he said. "Those guys upstairs are *SkyWakers*, just like us. We can't leave them. They're fam." He looked around the group, gauging their reaction.

Fish grunted in agreement. "That's what I've always loved about this game," he admitted. "It's a proper community. All that time we spent together online, sharing stories, having a laugh, made me feel like we were mates. Proper mates. Even better than my real-life friends, or my useless brothers."

"Word," Elite agreed.

Fish paused a moment, wanting to say more. "That's why I got so mad when I found out Casey Flow wasn't a boy," he continued. "It felt like everything we'd shared was fake."

"I'm really sorry," Casey said.

Fish shifted his weight from one foot to the other uncomfortably. Finally, he looked her in the eye. "Thing is, though, you were right," he confessed. "If I'd known you were a girl, I probably would have rage-quit or called you a noob and told you to play support instead of DPS. But the fact is, you're the best *SkyWake* player I've ever met."

He picked up the plasma rifle. His arms sagged

under its weight as he held it out like a peace offering for Casey to take.

"If your brother's still here, we can still rescue him," he said. "You lead and we'll follow. You're the shot caller, just like in the game."

Casey looked at the boys. She wasn't sure she deserved their belief in her.

"Fish is right," Brain said. "You're incredible with that rifle. I don't know how you're doing everything you're doing, but you've got …"

"Mad skillz," Elite said, finishing his sentence for him.

"Yeah," the others agreed.

Fish pushed the rifle at her, forcing her to take it. It felt good in her hands. It was true, she did seem to know how to use it. Whatever was happening to her today was giving her an edge. But would that be enough? She chewed her bottom lip, uncertainly.

"We've got no chance if we attack the Red Eyes head-on, have we?" she asked, turning to Brain.

Brain nodded. "I'd say it's less than five per cent. But it's like Elite said. It's not purely about numbers any more. We can't just stand around like these dummies." He waved his arm at the mannequins in their swimsuits and sun hats. "We've got to at least try to help."

Casey rested the barrel of the gun on her shoulder. With her free hand she reached out to the dog tags around her neck. She let her fingers run over the embossed letters of her dad's name, wondering what he would tell her to do.

It was an impossible choice: run away and leave Pete to be taken on the dropship, or die trying to getting him back.

"OK," she said after a moment. "We'll go upstairs and scavenge some weapons from the supply crates. Then we'll see what we can do. But if it's too dangerous, we should retreat back to the tunnel. We've lost enough people today."

She looked down at the gun she was holding and wished her hands would stop shaking.

24

WHISTLE WHILE YOU WORK

Pete was small, but he could run fast. He dashed through the Arcturian dropship, leaving the loadout bay behind. The ship's gloom worked in his favour. Every corridor was bathed in shadow, obscuring him from the pursuing Red Eyes.

He turned the corner and looked around, uncertain where to go next. Running blindly through the dropship didn't seem like much of a plan. He noticed a cluster of thick venting pipes that ran down from the ceiling and along the length of the floor. They were mounted on supports that lifted them off the ground. A control panel hung on the wall beside them. As Pete watched, the pipes released a cloud of gaseous green plasma. It hissed around the corridor, giving him an idea.

He tapped the control panel, trying to turn off the

supply of plasma to the vents. He didn't fancy getting a faceful. The control panel didn't respond to his touch and so, frustrated, Pete pulled the wires out. It sparked for a moment and then fell dead. The smell of burning electrical circuits filled his nostrils.

Behind him, Pete could hear his pursuers approaching. He rolled under the pipes, and, making himself as small as he could, he squeezed into the gap between them and the floor. He'd just got into position, lying on his belly in the gloom under the pipes, when two Red Eyes arrived. They stopped and looked around, wondering which way he'd run.

The pipes were warm to the touch and Pete guessed they were connected to the ship's engine system. The dropships were powered by a central plasma engine core that ran hot and was susceptible to blowing up if it wasn't kept at the right temperature. He'd learned that in the game.

And so far today, everything in the game was proving to be true.

He held his breath as the two Red Eye grunts searched the corridor. He lay on the ground under the pipes, his heart hammering in his chest as their boots walked right past his head. He prayed they wouldn't notice that the pipes weren't venting their regular clouds of green plasma or see the busted control panel on the wall.

One Red Eye growled something to the other in Arcturian. Pete tensed, expecting to be hauled out of his hiding place at any moment. But they marched on down the corridor and vanished around the corner.

He'd tricked them!

Pete allowed himself to take a breath. He felt small and scared. But more than that, he felt like a coward. He'd left Xander and the rest of Strike Force behind so he could save his own skin. He hadn't meant to run away; he just couldn't help himself. It had been a case of fight or flight. And flight had won. Big time.

He fought back tears, ashamed. If he couldn't fight, maybe he could still do something to help. Maybe he could save them some other way. But how?

If the Red Eyes were taking the gamers onto the dropship, they must be planning on leaving with them. Maybe Pete could sneak off the ship and find help. The thought of getting back outside into the sunlight and fresh air made his heart leap. He tried to tell himself it was because he wanted to help Xander. But deep down he knew it was because he was afraid of this dark, gloomy craft and the thought of where it might take him.

He heard a low hum as a drone sailed around the corner. He paused, wondering if it had been sent by the Red Eyes to find him, but no, it was an engineering drone, one of the many autonomous bots that kept the dropship running smoothly. It stopped at the pipes and scanned the control panel Pete had busted. Clearly the ship's systems had realized there was a problem and dispatched the drone to see what was going on. Pete watched as the machine extended a jointed metal spike towards the dead controls. It expertly removed the section of wall panel to reveal the wires that Pete had yanked out of place.

He guessed it would ignore him. Just to be sure, though, he stayed hidden. He'd wait until it had finished, then carry on.

The sound of footsteps jolted Pete back to his predicament. The Red Eyes were returning to the corridor. They clearly didn't believe he'd run on. He lay still under the nest of pipes as the aliens shouted instructions to one another. They were spreading out along the corridor, searching every corner.

He was busted.

He felt a shiver of dread creeping up his spine. What should he do? What should he do? What should he do?

He looked over at the drone. It was busily removing wall panels as it went about its repair job, oblivious to his presence. As the drone's spiked tool detached a section of venting, it revealed a gaping black hole that led into the ship's innards. The drone hovered over to the opening and flew inside. A moment later there was a crackle and a flicker of sparks as it began repairing the electrical wiring. The drone bleeped and chirruped to itself, like a builder whistling while he worked.

Pete stared at the Red Eyes. One carried a plasma rifle. Another had an energy sword. Another held some kind of tracking device and was sweeping it around as if he was trying to get a fix on a signal.

Pete looked down at the exo-suit he'd been kitted out with. Could there be a tracking device inside it? Some way for the Arcturians to keep tabs on their prisoners? In the game, your mini-map always showed the location of your squad mates. Still lying under the pipe, he unclipped the harness holding the armour in place and silently wriggled out of it.

The Red Eyes were drawing closer. The one with the tracking device was jabbing an excited finger in Pete's direction, one eye on the screen of his handheld device.

Pete knew it was time to move.

He rolled out from under the pipes, staying low and using the shadows as cover. He crawled into the vent, pushing past the drone as it finished up the repairs, and it bleeped as if complaining at his rudeness. Pete crept into the shadows. He watched as the Red Eyes found his exo-suit. One picked it up and waved it at the others angrily, shouting in annoyance that it was nothing more than a red herring. They seemed sure they'd lost him.

The drone gave out a satisfied beep and its soldering tool retracted into its body. It turned around in mid-air and stared at him, a light on its front flickering on and shining into his eyes.

He remained dead still, letting the light blind him. He didn't even dare close his eyes. The drone whistled something to itself and then, satisfied that nothing was amiss, turned again and headed out of the vent. A moment later it replaced the cover, sealing him inside.

Pete felt the darkness close in around him, and as it did, a growing sense of relief enveloped him. He realized he was trapped. That meant there was no way he could be a hero now.

For the first time in hours, he finally felt safe.

25

THE OLD TROJAN
PRISONER ROUTINE

The top floors of the shopping centre looked like an abandoned war zone. Broken glass and spent shell casings littered the marble tiles, leftovers from the battle between the aliens and Dreyfus's soldiers. A few clamshell-shaped energy shields stood here and there, flickering as their battery packs dwindled to empty. The balcony railings had been melted by plasma fire, leaving a cliff-edge drop into the atrium below. The Ghost Reapers stayed well away from the edge.

"How long do you think we've got before they take off?" Casey asked her teammates.

"I'm not sure," Brain said. "I guess they'll need to prep the ship first. But who knows how long that takes. They've rounded up all the gamers they wanted. It can't be long until they're gone."

Aware that time was running out, the group

hurried through the devastation. They crouched low as they ran, trying not to let the rubber soles of their trainers squeak on the polished marble floors in case any Red Eyes lurked in the shadows.

When they reached the purple supply crates, Casey tapped the glyphs on the touchscreen control panel of the first one she came to, just as she would if she was playing *SkyWake*. It unlocked and slid open with a swish and a futuristic bleep.

"I want an energy shield," Fish said elbowing his way to the front of the group. He was still carrying the yellow detonator under his arm. His face fell as he peered inside.

"It's empty!"

Brain joined him. "They must have cleared it out before they left," he groaned. Elite ran to the other crates and opened them. They were empty too.

Casey leaned against the first crate. Her head was spinning. Pete was upstairs on that strange alien craft. Alone, without her. Any minute now she would feel the building shake as the dropship took off, heading who knew where with her little brother on board. She stared into the empty supply crate, realizing what it meant.

It was over.

"We can't do anything without weapons," Brain said, voicing her thoughts. The rest of the boys shifted uncomfortably, waiting for someone to argue with him. But they all knew it was hopeless.

"Casey?" Elite asked.

She shook her head, unable to speak.

"We tried," Fish said. "We did that at least…" His voice trailed off into silence.

There was a heavy tread of footsteps behind them. Casey looked over the ruined balcony and saw a lone Red Eye heading up the escalators towards them. He hadn't seen them yet but it would only be a matter of time. She felt her body tense.

"Find some cover," she whispered to the boys, looking around for somewhere to conceal herself. There wasn't time to run across the balcony.

"There's nowhere to hide, yo," Elite whispered.

"Every man for himself!" Fish hissed, and dived into the empty supply crate, still cradling the detonator box. The lid bleeped and shut over him.

"Get behind the crate," Casey told the others, crouching behind it – although it was barely wide enough for the three of them.

The Red Eye clattered up the stairs. His movements were slightly jerky, as if his power suit wasn't working properly. He crossed the floor, his heavy combat boots crushing glass shards and metal shell casings from the earlier fire-fight.

Casey poked her head around the side of the supply crate as he approached. There was something strange about his armour. As he got closer, she could see that it was covered in strips of some kind, silver strips. They almost looked like duct tape. At least, she noted, he wasn't carrying a weapon. Maybe they still had a chance. She checked her plasma rifle was charged and lifted it to her shoulder in readiness.

The Red Eye headed across the balcony and stopped in front of the crate, his red mechanical eyes burning bright in his helmet. The boys behind the crate squirmed and wriggled in panic, trying to make themselves as small as possible. Elite's scuffed trainers were sticking out on one side of the crate and the top of Brain's head was visible above it. Casey's finger curled around the trigger of her rifle.

The Red Eye cocked his head on one side. "That's the worst hiding place ever," he said in his deep voice. It took Casey a second to realize what was so strange about it.

He was speaking English!

She stuck her head out and stared at the alien. His

armour was badly battered and, now that he was up close, she could see it really was held together by duct tape.

It was, she realized with a jolt, Scratch's armour. But Scratch had been stretchered upstairs…

"I guess you're wondering who I am," the Red Eye said. He put his black-gloved hands to his head and pulled his dented helmet off to reveal a face they all recognized.

"Cheeze!" Casey yelled in surprise and delight.

"I always hate it when you guys play without me," the boy said with a grin.

Elite and Brain popped up from behind the supply crate and ran towards him, whooping and hollering with excitement. Casey stared in astonishment before joining them in a group hug.

"What's going on?" a muffled voice asked from inside the crate. "Are you being murdered? Guys? Are you there? I'm stuck. There aren't any buttons on the inside."

"Someone should let Fish out," Casey said.

"Do we have to?" Cheeze asked with a smile.

"After you got away, the Red Eyes stormed the control room," Cheeze told them a few moments later, as he brought them up to speed with everything that had happened. "They took the lieutenant. But they left me alone when they saw I couldn't stand without my wheelchair. I guess the Red Eye army doesn't believe in equal opportunities."

"What about Wilson and Tucker?"

"Last I saw, they were still knocked out by the tarantulas' venom. After the Red Eyes left, I patched this suit together and hacked into it. It's controlled by my nervous system, so even though I can't move my legs, I can use it to get around and – *ta-dah!* – alien mobility aid."

He did a little shimmy in celebration then quickly stopped, his face creased in pain.

"Are you OK?" Casey asked, grabbing his arm.

"It hurts a bit. I've been in my wheelchair so long, my body's not used to standing upright. It feels really weird to be up here at your height. But also cool! And I couldn't just leave you guys out here."

"Hashtag impressed." Brain nodded.

"So," Cheeze asked, "what's the game plan?"

"There isn't one," Fish admitted. "We came up here looking for weapons but all the supply crates are empty. There's nothing except for these things."

He pulled a couple of neck shackles from the

supply crate he'd been hiding in and held them aloft, despairing.

"What you going to do, make yourselves into prisoners and save the Red Eyes the trouble?" Cheeze snorted.

There was a pause. Then Casey's eyes lit up. "Actually," she said, "that's exactly what we should do."

The boys all turned to look at her in surprise. She had clearly had an idea. If she'd been a cartoon character, she would have had a light bulb hanging over her head.

"Why do I get the feeling I'm not going to like this one bit?" Fish muttered.

"Trust me, Fish," Casey told him, "you're going to *love* this plan."

By the time they reached the top of the escalator, Casey and the boys were shuffling along in a line with shackles around their necks. Cheeze, with his helmet back on and Casey's plasma rifle in his hands, guarded them as they stepped out onto the rooftop.

"I hate this plan," Fish whined, tugging the shackle around his neck. Before they set off, Cheeze had opened up the devices and worked out what they were for and how to deactivate them. Even so, the Ghost

Reapers still felt apprehensive about wearing them. Fortunately, they'd only need to fool the Red Eyes long enough to get on board. Once they were on the ship, they could get rid of them.

Crossing the roof towards the waiting dropship, the boys stared up at it in wonder. Casey, however, peered over the side of the building to the car park below. Tanks and artillery guns were lining up on the other side of the force field. It looked like everyone in charge was convinced this was an invasion. By the time the authorities worked out what was really happening, the dropship would have dusted off with its prisoners.

They'd decided to leave the detonator they'd taken from Dreyfus inside the supply crate. Cheeze had scrambled the lock to keep it safe. It gave her some small comfort to know that, whatever happened next, no one would be blowing up the shopping centre today.

She thought of her mum down there in the crowd, terrified and anxious. She longed to be able to tell her what was happening. But there was no way she could face her without Pete. She had to get him back. She balled her hands into fists, digging her nails into her palms. She would find a way to stop the ship from taking off.

She had to.

*   *   *

At the ramp, the Red Eyes had just finished loading Scratch's gurney, rushing her inside. Dreyfus, still a prisoner, was next in line to board the ship. Casey wondered why they'd bothered taking him. Perhaps they were planning an intricate act of revenge. What would be more cruel than sending this human soldier to fight on Hosin? Placing the proud military man on an alien battlefield, where he didn't know the weapons or the enemy, would be his worst nightmare.

The Red Eye grunts stopped and stared when they saw Cheeze approaching them with his captives. He raised his hand, holding it sideways across his chest in the clenched fist greeting that the Arcturians used as a salute.

"*Whar hef gecht?*" one of the alien soldiers demanded.

Cheeze tapped his helmet's mouthpiece and shook his head as if it wasn't working.

"*Pran imboci,*" the other Red Eye said to his buddy as they looked Cheeze's battered, duct-taped armour up and down in a mocking manner. They seemed highly amused by the state of it. They stepped forwards and scanned the teams' badges with their lasers.

Casey, wearing Cheeze's **COMPETITOR** badge,

tried not to panic as the laser flashed over her. There was a bleep as the badge was accepted.

The alien soldiers hesitated a moment, looking at the group uncertainly. At first, Casey thought it was because they were so late to arrive. All the other gamers were already inside. But then she realized the flaw in her plan.

A full *SkyWake* squad should be five players.

But there were only four.

There was a pause as the two Red Eyes conferred in their strange language. The boys exchanged frightened glances. Fish looked like he might be about to make a run for it, but Casey gripped his elbow and shook her head. The last thing they could afford to do now was break cover. They had to play it cool.

Cheeze stepped forward. His step was jerky and awkward. He raised his arm and pointed across at Dreyfus, who was waiting to go up the ramp. The soldier stared back at them, pulling defiantly at the shock shackle around his neck.

The Red Eyes looked at Dreyfus then back at Cheeze, who jabbed his finger at Dreyfus again. Casey realized what he was doing. He was telling them to make Dreyfus part of their squad. The Red Eyes talked amongst themselves, clearly discussing the merits of this plan. Finally, one of the aliens nodded and ushered Casey and the others over to where Dreyfus was standing.

"I might have known you'd be captured too," the lieutenant muttered as the Ghost Reapers drew near. "What have you done with my detonator?"

"It's gone," Casey whispered, keeping her voice low. Dreyfus's body stiffened with anger.

"You stupid girl!" he hissed. "You've damned us all."

A Red Eye shoved the butt of his plasma rifle between Dreyfus's shoulder blades, pushing him up the ramp into the dropship. The teammates were led behind him. As they stepped up the ramp, it started to close. There was a hiss as it sealed itself shut.

Casey felt a sense of dread creeping up her spine.

What if Dreyfus was right?

What if she'd just made the worst mistake of her life?

26

IN THE BELLY OF THE BEAST

The interior of the dropship was gloomy and unwelcoming. Strange alien glyphs glowed on control consoles on the walls and, now and then, thin clouds of green plasma gas burst from the vents in the floor. It was like being inside a strange, toxic factory.

Casey knew the layout well. In *SkyWake*, the dropship map was the backdrop for a last man standing mode. One team was a squad of Red Eyes trapped on board a grounded ship. The other team played the Squids storming the stricken vessel to capture it. With limited ammo and no respawns, the map encouraged both teams to play tactically, hiding and sneaking through the different levels of the ship until they had eliminated all of the enemy team. But there was a twist: the Red Eyes had to protect the engine's cooling systems from the Squid attackers. If the four cooling pumps went offline, the dropship wouldn't be able to take off.

The guards escorting them paused a moment. Casey took the opportunity to look around. She never liked the map much. It was too claustrophobic; too enclosed. But Pete had always adored it. In the early days, when *SkyWake* was first released, he'd discovered a hidden engineering vent that crisscrossed the ship. He loved to crawl in there, holding a psi grenade, and drop it onto the Squids as they slithered beneath him. After a while, the hidden vent became common knowledge and the tactic lost its effectiveness.

Remembering the map, though, had given Casey a plan. If they could get to the cooling pumps, they could disable the dropship and stop it from taking off. All they needed was to get inside and then overpower their guards. With Cheeze in disguise, they had a decent chance. It was just a matter of timing.

As they were marched through the ship, Casey told the others her idea. She made sure to keep her voice to a whisper, even though she knew the Red Eyes couldn't speak English.

"You know," Brain said, after he'd digested her plan, "you're making a huge assumption..."

"What do you mean?" Casey asked, her voice low.

"Who says the real dropship's layout is the same as in *SkyWake*?" her friend asked. "Maybe there aren't even any cooling pumps."

It was a good question, although it was one Casey wished he hadn't asked. "Everything else has been the same so far," Casey said, trying to soothe his fears. "The weapons, the Red Eyes…"

"Who even designed the game, anyway?" Fish hissed beside her.

"It must be someone snatched by the Red Eyes," Brain said.

Elite looked around nervously, not really listening. "This is taking too long."

"Just stick to the plan," Casey told them. "As soon as we get to the loadout bay, we'll make a break for it and grab some weapons. Then we'll head for the engine room and take the cooling pumps offline. It's going to work."

PSSSH-FSSH!

The Ghost Reapers jumped as a thin green cloud of plasma billowed out of a nearby vent, enveloping them in its bitter smell. It made Casey's throat sting and her eyes water. They all coughed, except Cheeze and the Red Eyes, who were protected from the noxious gas in their powered armour. Casey stumbled forwards, dabbing her face on her sleeve and blinking hard, momentarily blinded.

That was why she didn't see the danger ahead until it was too late.

Outside the entrance to the loadout bay stood an overseer commander and two Red Eye grunts in white armour. Casey recognized them as medics. The three of them were standing around the gurney, which was now parked in the middle of the corridor.

Lying on it was Scratch.

The alien screeched in pain, tubes and drips hanging out of her body. Her condition must have worsened on the way to the medical bay, because they seemed to be performing some kind of emergency procedure in the corridor to keep her alive. They were encasing her in sections of new armour as quickly as possible.

The medics worked furiously, paying the Ghost Reapers little attention. But Scratch saw them coming. Her lips curled into a sneer as they approached. Casey prayed that she wouldn't notice Cheeze's battered armour – *her* armour – and raise the alarm.

The boys passed the gurney one by one. When it was Casey's turn, she swallowed hard and kept her head down, careful not to look in the direction of the injured alien. She counted the floor vents beneath her feet as she walked. One, two, three, four... She was almost at the loadout bay door when she felt something cold and scaly against her wrist.

She let out a yelp as Scratch's talon-like hand grabbed her arm and turned her to face the gurney. Panicked, Casey tried to pull herself free. But Scratch tightened her grip, refusing to let go. They stared at each other for a moment and Casey felt a chill run through her. It wasn't the hatred in Scratch's eyes, nor the way her talons dug into her wrist that terrified her. It was the sound the alien made.

Her strange mouth moved jerkily as she struggled to voice English syllables she'd never spoken before.

"Game over," she hissed awkwardly in English, repeating the words Casey had said to her in Starbucks earlier that day. Then she made a horrid croaking noise.

It was, Casey realized in horror, the Arcturian equivalent of mocking laughter.

27

I HEAR YOU KNOCKING, BUT YOU CAN'T COME IN

What happened next was something of a blur. Casey yanked her wrist free from Scratch's grip, ignoring the pain as the alien's black talons ripped the skin on her arm and drew blood.

"Run!" she yelled to the boys.

At the same moment, the overseer leading them reached for the clicker on his belt, ready to shock the teammates into submission. But the only person who got shocked was Dreyfus. The overseer stared in surprise as the Ghost Reapers, in deactivated shackles, remained completely unharmed.

Panicked, the Red Eye escorts brought their plasma rifles up. Cheeze opened fire on them first, catching them off guard thanks to his alien suit. As the gunfire erupted, the medics dived for cover and Scratch fell to the floor, writhing and thrashing in fury.

"Get inside the loadout bay!" Casey yelled, dragging Dreyfus with her, gritting her teeth at the jolt of lingering electricity she got when she touched him. The boys didn't need further prompting, and dived through the blast doors. Cheeze, firing over his shoulder, was the last one in before the heavy doors shut like steel jaws. He blasted the control panel with his gun, sealing them inside. There were muffled thuds and shouts as the Red Eyes hammered on the other side.

"How long do you think those will hold them?" Casey asked. An alarm sounded somewhere deeper inside the dropship, shrill and insistent.

"Not long enough," Cheeze said. He pulled the Arcturian helmet off his head and leaned against the wall, panting. "I'll be OK," he told Casey, waving away her concern. "But this suit isn't designed for humans. I'm really missing my wheelchair right now."

Just then, there was a tremor beneath their feet. The ship seemed to rumble and shake and a cloud of green plasma vented from the floors and walls, momentarily engulfing them in its acidic mist. They clung on to whatever they could as the whole ship seemed to lurch sideways. It only lasted a moment, but they all guessed what it meant.

"Tell me we didn't just take off..." Fish whispered.

"This is bad," Elite said, panicked. "How are we ever gonna get out of here now?"

On the floor, Dreyfus was just coming to after his shock. He looked pale and weak. Cheeze removed the shock collar from around his neck.

"Getting us locked in here was your plan?" the soldier asked Casey, his voice dripping with sarcasm. "You should let me take charge."

"You don't know anything about how *SkyWake* works," she replied, surprised by the steel in her tone. "You're in our world now."

Casey looked around the shadowy loadout bay, noticing the conveyor belts. She knew from her hours playing *SkyWake* exactly what lay at the end of them. It was the ship's central gravity well where the drop pods were prepped before being launched.

On the far side of the blast doors there was a clatter and some muffled shouts in Arcturian. Then a shower of sparks began to spew from under the doors. The Red Eyes outside the loadout bay were using some kind of plasma torch on it. A hot orange line appeared halfway down and slowly inched its way across the metal.

"What are we going to do?" Fish asked. The boys

looked at Casey expectantly. Dreyfus too. She took a breath. She could do this.

"If the ship's already taken off, we're too late to cut the cooling pumps," she told them. "We need to get back to Earth."

"How?" Fish asked. "Hijack the ship and turn it around?"

"We're going to have to hot-drop," Casey told them.

"What does that mean?" asked Dreyfus.

"Trust me, bruv, you don't want to know," Elite muttered, shaking his head in despair.

"The ship's drop pods are designed for planet fall," Brain told the lieutenant. "We can blast back to Earth in them."

"Not just us," Casey corrected him. "If we can get control of the pods, we can rescue all the gamers."

Dreyfus looked at her in surprise. He seemed almost impressed.

"I'll work on overriding the pods," Cheeze said, heading over to the loadout bay's control console and grabbing a seat in front of it. He was glad to be sitting down; the alien suit was too uncomfortable. "If I can find the launch command, we can get everyone out of here." He pulled an Arcturian hacking tool from his belt and got started.

"What about those Red Eyes?" Fish asked, nervously eyeing the blast doors. The aliens were still cutting through the metal, slowly but surely. Sparks showered left and right, dropping into the floor grilles like glowing orange embers before they cooled and went out.

"We'll have to hold them back until Cheeze is ready," Casey said. "Everyone, grab some weapons."

The boys fanned out into the loadout bay. It didn't take them long to find the bay's stash of weapons. They ran to the racks and pulled down hardware they recognized from *SkyWake*. Fish grabbed exo-suits and helmets for everyone as well as an energy shield baton for himself. Brain took an energy sword and a med tool, weighing both in his hands. Elite took a long, narrow sniper rifle that was the length of a broomstick.

"This is sweet," he whistled, peering down the rifle's scope and watching as it synced up to the display on his helmet visor.

While they tooled up, Cheeze tapped away at the alien console, trying to decipher its strange glyphs. Dreyfus hung on to the back of his seat, still groggy from the electric shock. He watched as Cheeze pulled up screen after screen of data then stopped in surprise. The gamer took a deep breath.

"Casey, you need to see this…"

On the screen was a map of the drop pods in the ship's hold. It showed the banks of pods, each with a soldier inside. Vital signs – heartbeat, rate of breathing, brain activity – scrolled across the screen alongside a pod symbol marked with the gamertag of the person inside. One pod flashed red: CASEY FLOW.

"It's Pete!" Casey cried, excited. "He must still be wearing my ID badge." She stared at the screen, unable to believe her eyes. "Is he OK?" she asked. "Can we speak to him?"

Cheeze didn't reply.

"What is it?" Casey demanded, scared. She could sense something was wrong. She looked again at the screen. The flashing red drop pod symbol suddenly seemed ominous. None of the other pods were flashing like that.

"There are no readings coming from his pod," Cheeze explained. "No heartbeat. No vital signs. Nothing."

"But that means he's…" Casey couldn't finish her sentence. She flushed, angry. "No! It can't be. There's just a problem with the system. A glitch or something."

She looked across the loadout bay and started to

head out to find her brother. Cheeze tried to grab her arm, but she shrugged him off.

"Don't let them inside," she ordered her teammates, indicating the blast doors where the Red Eyes were still cutting through. "I'll be back as quick as I can." She caught Dreyfus watching her and expected him to try and stop her. But he didn't. He just nodded.

"Good luck," he said.

Casey turned on her heel and ran. The shadows engulfed her instantly.

28

HIDE AND SEEK

The great thing about the exo-suit, Casey realized as she ran, was the way it augmented your body. Everything still moved just like it always did, but the suit's metal rods and joints made her faster and more powerful. The plasma rifle in her hands no longer felt too heavy for her, and when she vaulted over a railing that separated the loadout bay from the gravity well, it was totally effortless. The exo-suit's servo-motors gave her added power to make the jump while its inbuilt dampeners cushioned the impact as she landed.

The well sat in the centre of the dropship on the far side of the loadout bay. It was a vast circular funnel that ran five storeys deep, through the belly of the ship. On the curved walls of the well, stacked in rows, were hundreds of drop pods. Each held a single gamer, kitted out with an exo-suit and weapons. The kidnapped kids stood motionless, their faces blank and their eyes glassy as marbles. If any of them noticed her approach, they gave no sign.

As Casey took in the sheer scale of it all, a huge robot arm moved gracefully across the well. It placed a final drop pod in position, slotting it into a gap between the others. Casey knew that when the time came, these pods would tumble like counters out of a Connect 4 rack, dropping from the ship's belly and into the atmosphere of whatever planet lay beneath them. It was a formidable assault strategy, and if the game's backstory also turned out to be true, it had allowed the Red Eyes to invade planet after planet.

Cheeze's voice crackled in her ear, coming through the comms system in the helmet of her exo-suit. It was like being back in game chat.

"You should be able to see Pete's location on your mini-map," he told her.

In the corner of her helmet's visor display, she saw a map like the ones in *SkyWake*. There was something comforting about its familiarity. The location of Pete's drop pod was a flashing red dot.

"I've got it," she replied, running down the metal stairs that ringed the circular walls. Pete should be at the very bottom of the well. She dashed past the other pods, thinking of all the other shopping centres around the world that had been targeted today. The Red Eyes must be building a global army to attack the Squids' homeworld. A final push to take over Hosin once and for all.

As she sprinted along the final walkway on the lowest level of the well, she hurried her step, watching the countdown on her helmet visor as it tracked the remaining distance to Pete.

Ten metres, five metres, two metres … *here!*

The visor silhouetted the pod in front of her, highlighting it so she couldn't miss it. She hammered her fist against its side.

"Pete. I'm here. Pete!"

There was no answer. Panicked, she wiped the frosted condensation that had formed over the pod's viewing window and peered inside. He had to be alive. He just had to be. She let out a strangled cry of despair.

"It's empty!" she yelled into her helmet mic, her chest heaving.

"It can't be," Cheeze's voice said. "The system says—"

"Then the system's wrong," Casey snapped. "He's not here."

She checked the pods next to the empty one, and recognized some of the kids from Strike Force.

"Xander!" she screamed, hammering on his pod. "Where's Pete?"

The YouTuber didn't respond. His eyes were glazed. Casey wasn't even sure if he knew she was there. She looked back at Pete's empty drop pod, unable to believe that the whole of this had been for nothing. She'd come all that way to find him! Maybe something had happened to him. Maybe he was already dead.

She steadied herself against the empty pod. She felt as though she was going to pass out. She hadn't eaten anything since breakfast and her body was telling her it couldn't go on much longer.

No, she told herself, *this isn't over.* There hadn't been any vital signs on the system because her brother wasn't in the pod. If he wasn't in the pod, he must be somewhere else.

She was jolted back to the present by the sound of Cheeze's words crackling in her ear again.

"Casey, we need you! They're coming inside."

By the time Casey got back to the loadout bay, the Red Eyes had finished cutting a rectangular hatch in the middle of the blast doors. As the last of the sparks died and went out, there was an ominous silence.

"What are they waiting for?" Fish snapped.

A few seconds ticked past. Still nothing.

"How long until we can release the pods?" Casey asked Cheeze.

"Five more minutes," her teammate called over his shoulder, his fingers clattering over the console's keyboard at lightning speed.

"You'll never hold them that long," Dreyfus said flatly.

"Yes, we will," Casey told him firmly. "We just need to play our game roles. Fish, get your shield up. Brain, be ready to heal. Elite, find a sniper spot."

The team rolled into action, buoyed by the authority in Casey's voice. There was something familiar about it, something that they recognized from the hours they'd spent playing *SkyWake* together. Looking at her, though, her teammates could also see how different she was. She was no longer the same girl who'd arrived in the shopping centre that morning too shy to reveal herself for fear they'd reject her.

If she felt the change in herself, Casey didn't show it. She was consumed by a million different thoughts, her mind racing to form a strategy before the Red Eyes breached the doors. If the Ghost Reapers couldn't keep the enemy soldiers back, there was no way she would ever find Pete.

She looked around, considering the best position to take up. There were four metal pillars opposite the main doors that would give her good cover. She ran behind the first one, her plasma rifle poking around it. She was surprised to notice that, for the first time today, her hands weren't shaking as she hefted the gun.

She was ready for this.

The boys followed her instructions to the letter.

Fish stepped forward and activated his shield baton. A horizontal rectangle of blue energy extended out in front of him, creating a barrier between his friends and the blast doors. He planted one leg behind him like a taekwondo fighter in standing stance and heard his exo-suit's servomotors whizz and whirr as they tightened, rooting him to the spot. He felt as immovable as an oak tree.

Behind the shield, Brain stood ready with his energy sword. Dreyfus crouched low by a stack of supply crates. Brain had shown him how to use a plasma pistol and he pointed the strange-looking weapon on the blast doors. Meanwhile, Elite was climbing a ladder onto a gantry above the loadout bay.

The height made it the perfect sniping spot.

"It's just like last man standing," Elite whispered on the comms as he lifted his scope to his eye and watched the blast doors.

No one replied, too focussed for chit-chat. The silence seemed to stretch on for ever. Then, all of a sudden, there was a heavy clang as a Red Eye boot kicked the door and the rectangular panel toppled forwards. It hit the floor and lay there like a tombstone.

"Here they come," Casey said into her helmet mic. "Make every shot count."

The shooting started immediately as a squad of Red Eyes blasted at them from the corridor. Fish's shield crackled and rippled as it soaked up plasma damage like a sponge. Elite's sniper rifle cracked in intermittent bursts as he lined up his targets, moving in and out of the shadows between shots. A Red Eye went down, his armoured helmet smoking.

"They call me sniper elite, cos I can't be beat," the boy's voice rapped over the comms. *"One shot in the head and you'll be dead."*

"Stop showing off," Casey warned, crouched behind her pillar. She released a barrage of fire through Fish's shield, distracting the Red Eyes from zeroing in on

Elite's position. She heard the *pop, pop, pop* of a plasma pistol across the loadout bay and guessed that Dreyfus was doing the same.

"Shield's at sixty per cent," Fish warned, clocking the flashing counter on his helmet display as the shield took hit after hit.

Casey fired again, dropping another alien who tried to breach the doors. The Red Eyes had cut it small and it was hard for them to get through without being hit. The alien's comrades pulled him back into the corridor to get patched up by the medics. More quickly arrived to take his place.

Casey wondered if Scratch was back on her feet yet. Would she come through the door looking for revenge? She pushed the thought out of her mind.

Without warning, there was a lull in the shooting. Casey and the boys instinctively took the opportunity to reload, all except Fish, who kept his shield up in case it was a ploy by the Red Eyes. The shield would recharge if he deactivated it, but he wasn't about to chance it. Not just yet.

"How much longer for the pods?" Casey yelled, looking over at Cheeze. He still had the hacking tool in his hand, its beam scrambling the console's systems as it tried to gain full access.

"I'm on the last layer of security. Just hold them back a little longer."

"Any sign of Pete?" she asked, although she knew what his answer would be.

"Nothing," Cheeze answered, shaking his head. "It's like he's vanished."

"He must be here somewhere," Brain said over the comms. "How many hiding places can there be on a ship like this?"

Casey exhaled hard, trying to fight back her panic. "He's been running away from me all day," she whispered, remembering how the day had started. "He didn't want me to babysit him at the tournament and I almost lost him in the crowds when we first got there. He's so small he can wriggle his way into all kinds of…"

She stopped mid-sentence.

"All kinds of what?" Elite asked.

"Small spaces! He's great at getting into small spaces. He even does it in *SkyWake*, on this map."

"And…?" prompted Fish.

"Last man standing is his favourite game mode," Casey continued, her voice rising as she joined up the dots. "He goes into the vents with a psi grenade…"

"On it," Cheeze replied, catching on. "Scanning the ventilation system now."

Casey held her breath. If Pete had disappeared once he was inside the dropship, he had to be in the vents. He knew every centimetre of them from the game.

"I've got a heat signature," Cheeze shouted. "It's in the cooling tower above the loadout bay."

Casey couldn't believe what she was hearing. Was it possible...? But she had no time to give it any more thought as the Red Eyes opened fire again from the corridor. Casey saw that they were now being led by Scratch, who, back in fresh armour but without a helmet, was shouting instructions at them in her alien tongue.

Everyone in the loadout bay ducked for cover, except Fish, who stood firm with his shield protecting them all.

"I've got to get Pete!" Casey yelled, glancing at the gantry above the loadout bay. The cooling vents were situated up there, above Elite's sniper spot.

"Shield's going down any minute," Fish called as the energy field cracked, flickered and began to die. He didn't want to get stuck out in the open when it went offline. Casey dived low as a blast of plasma fire ate into the pillar she was hiding behind.

"We can't hold them back without you, Casey," Brain shouted. "We don't have enough firepower."

He was right. They needed an assault player down here. If Casey abandoned the boys, they'd be overrun. But if she didn't reach Pete now, she'd never get him to a drop pod before their escape.

She felt a wave of despair.

How could she choose between her brother and her team?

"Yo, Casey," said a voice over the comms. "I've got you."

It was Elite. Her scrawny teammate had climbed up towards the ceiling of the loadout bay. At first, Casey thought he was trying to get to higher ground. But then she saw that he'd set his sniper rifle aside. He ripped the cover off a vent hatch, ready to scramble inside.

"You can't!" she said. "You hate small spaces!"

"Yes, I can," Elite replied over the comms channel. "I owe you, for the lift." He flashed her a cocky salute from the gantry, drew his back-up plasma pistol from the holster on the hip of his exo-suit, and vanished into the vents.

Casey felt a lump forming in her throat. But there was no time to get emotional – a whole squad of Red Eyes was storming into the loadout bay. And Scratch was at the front.

29

IN FULL FLOW

The Red Eyes stormed into the loadout bay, tossing four plasma grenades ahead of them. They bounced over the floor grilles towards Fish, landing at his feet with a metallic clatter. He dropped to one knee, lowering his energy shield to the floor, and blocked them like a wicket-keeper stopping a ball at a cricket match.

They triggered simultaneously in a flash of green plasma. The shield took the force of the blast, but the impact ran its battery packs down to empty. As it died, Fish was knocked off his feet by the shock wave.

Seizing the moment, Scratch hollered at her squad to charge forwards. The first Red Eye, a tank just like Fish, ran out in front and activated his shield to protect the others behind him.

The Red Eyes had breached the loadout bay.

Casey swallowed hard and gazed around. Brain was pulling Fish to safety, while Dreyfus covered them both with his plasma pistol. It was so puny it was next to useless. Cheeze was still trying to hack the control systems to release the pods so they could drop back to Earth. But it didn't look like he'd be able to do it in time.

This is how you die, Casey thought to herself. *You and your friends.* She felt tears welling up in her eyes. She couldn't let it end like this. She couldn't let today have all been for nothing.

She stared at the plasma rifle in her hands. It was all that stood between her and defeat. It was just her and a gun against the aliens, with nothing but four pillars to hide behind as the Red Eyes advanced. She felt a sudden wave of déjà vu, as if she'd been here before.

"It's just like *Space Invaders*," she muttered, realizing why it seemed so familiar. She was the lone gun turret trying to protect everyone, darting from base to base as the aliens rained down fire on her. A wave of calm washed over her. She knew how to do this better than anyone.

Go with the flow, Casey.

She felt her mind snap into focus. Everything else fell away. This, she realized, must be like the Long

Walk that her dad had told her about. But, before she knew it, even that thought was gone and her mind completely emptied. All her doubt had vanished.

She felt totally alert. Totally alive.

She dived across the space between the pillars and dropped to one knee. The rifle was already in her hands, its stock against her shoulder, aimed at the Red Eyes. She watched it shoot out a ball of plasma that sailed past the Red Eyes' shield tank and hit one of the aliens full in the chest. He fell to the ground, his power armour smoking and sparking.

Move. Stop. Shoot.

Casey rolled to the next pillar, confusing the Red Eyes. The aliens' shield tank spun around, trying to keep track of her. She popped out of cover and blasted them again. She was fighting with a new-found confidence, the exo-suit augmenting every move she took.

She was here, in the moment.

This was flow ... in real life.

Scratch shrieked as Casey rolled from behind a pillar and dropped another Red Eye. She was clearly infuriated that this girl seemed to be everywhere, all at once, impossible to stop.

Casey grabbed a second behind the next pillar and

caught her breath. The touchscreen on her rifle was flashing; she was low on power. There was one good shot left in it. She had to make it count.

She looked upwards, wondering where Elite was. She could do with his sniper rifle to cover her right now. As she stared up at the shadowy ceiling of the loadout bay, an idea hit her.

"Brain!" she yelled. "I need a distraction. Throw a grenade."

"I've only got one," Brain replied, terrified by the Red Eyes' relentless advance. "It's not enough to do anything."

"Just throw it!!" Casey yelled, louder than she'd ever yelled anything before.

She crouched low behind the pillar, waiting for her teammate to toss the projectile. The grenade landed in front of the tank, and Scratch and the other Red Eyes ducked behind the shield as it exploded, its blast effortlessly absorbed by the energy field.

Scratch smirked and shouted at her troops to make a final advance. She was convinced they'd won. As the squad moved forwards, Casey swung out from behind the pillar. She aimed her plasma rifle at the ceiling and pulled the trigger hard, draining every last bit of energy out of the gun's battery packs. A shining orb of plasma flew through the air over the Red Eyes' heads. Scratch grinned, thinking Casey's shot had gone wide just like it had done in Starbucks.

"*Rth'he calfu mort—*" the alien started to say, her black eyes flashing with mockery. Before she could finish her sentence, though, there was a crash as the structure above the blast doors collapsed, its supports destroyed by Casey's plasma burst. The walkway crashed to the floor right in front of the advancing Red Eyes, blocking their way. The last thing Casey saw as the twisted metal hit the ground was Scratch shouting furiously at her troops. Then the Red Eyes were gone, cut off behind the makeshift barricade that now separated them from the Reapers.

A sudden hush descended over the loadout bay as the dust settled.

"Is everyone OK?" Casey asked. The boys looked at one another, not quite able to believe what they'd just seen.

"That was incredible!" Cheeze exclaimed.

Elite's voice interrupted them on the comms. "I need some help over here, yo."

There was a clatter from a vent on the gantry above them and Elite crawled out. Behind him came a smaller figure.

"Pete!" Casey cried.

The two boys jumped down. Casey ran over and grabbed her little brother as he reached the ground.

"Casey!" he grinned. "I knew you'd come for me." He buried his face into her embrace.

"I thought I'd lost you for ever," Casey said, tears streaming down her cheeks. "Are you hurt?" She broke her hug to check him over, suddenly panicked.

"I'm OK," he said sheepishly.

"Are you sure?" She ran her hands over him, as if unable to believe he was really there.

"I tried to fight back," he told her, his voice cracking, "but I wasn't brave enough. Xander came up with a plan and I—" Ashamed and exhausted, he couldn't finish his story. He burst into tears. "I let everyone down."

"You're safe now," Casey whispered, stroking the back of his head as she'd seen their mum do. "I love you, little brother. I won't let anything happen to you ever again. And I promise I won't let you pretend to be me again, either."

She felt him half laugh, half sob against her chest. For a moment, Casey imagined they were back home in their kitchen, just the two of them, with their mum coming home from her shift at the hospital with a Saturday night takeaway, just like she always did. Her heart ached for that to be real.

"I don't know what I would have done if I'd lost you too," she whispered to Pete, thinking of how much she missed their dad. She hugged him all the tighter.

She felt someone touch her shoulder apologetically.

"Casey, we need to move," said Cheeze.

Pete blinked at Cheeze, surprised to see him without his wheelchair. He took in the rest of the Reapers, all of them now wearing exo-suits and carrying *SkyWake* weapons.

"You guys look badass," he said, impressed and a little envious.

The Ghost Reapers took a moment and stared at one another. It was true. They did.

"We came, we saw, we …" Brain started to say.

"… kicked alien butt." Elite finished the sentence for him. They fist-bumped.

Pete looked on, wishing he was part of the team. Casey, sensing his disappointment, put her arm around his shoulder and gave him a squeeze. She looked over at the collapsed walkway. She could hear the Red Eyes on the other side of it, trying to find a way through. It wouldn't stop them for long.

"The drop pods are ready," Cheeze said. "It's time to get out of here and go home."

"Hold on," Fish said, suddenly sceptical. "How sure are you about this?" He looked at the team questioningly. "Do you even know where we are?"

Cheeze squinted at the visuals on the control console. "I think we're in orbit," he said.

"You *think* we're in orbit?" Fish mocked, his voice dripping with sarcasm. "Well, sorry, pal, but I'd rather you *knew* for certain before we blast out into space in a bunch of tin cans."

"We're definitely in orbit," Cheeze said, sounding more confident this time. "That's the symbol. Look." He tapped a strange glyph on the console screen.

"He's right," Brain said, peering over his shoulder. "It's the symbol that appears in the game when it's safe to planet-drop. If we blast off now, the drop pods will take us back to Earth."

Casey looked around the group, sensing how anxious everyone was feeling. She didn't want to be blasted out of the dropship either, but it was their only hope of escaping. It wouldn't take the Red Eyes long to find a way through the rubble blocking their path.

"We can do this, team," she told them. "We just need to—"

There was a sudden clatter above them.

"What was that?" Fish asked.

They looked up at the vent, the one Elite and Pete had climbed out of just a few minutes before, to see about a dozen tarantulas spilling from it, their sleek metal bodies glinting in the gloom. They skittered over one another as they burst out onto the gantry. They paused a moment, looking at the team down below. Then they started to scurry down the walls of the loadout bay.

"You've gotta be kidding me," Fish said, despairing. "Don't they ever give up?"

"Run!" Casey shouted. "Get to the drop pods."

The Ghost Reapers sprinted through the shadows to the far side of the loadout bay with the tarantulas in pursuit. Casey kept hold of Pete's hand, dragging him with her, determined not to lose him again.

When they reached the gravity well, they found a row of empty pods, open and waiting for them. Cheeze had got everything ready. Each pod was just big enough to hold one person, standing upright. Dreyfus, Elite, Fish and Brain climbed inside and the pods sealed tight behind them with a hiss.

"Where's Cheeze?" Casey asked.

"There!" Pete cried, pointing to a figure running

awkwardly down the gantry with three tarantulas nipping at his heels.

"I've set the launch sequence!" Cheeze yelled as he approached. "We need to get into the pods."

Casey nodded and pushed Pete towards the nearest one. He fell backwards into it and a harness locked around his body, holding him tight against the pod's padded interior. The lid started to close, but Casey stopped it with her hand. She reached under her exo-suit and yanked their dad's dog tags from around her neck.

"For luck," she said, throwing them to her brother. He caught them and closed his fist around them. "Dad would be so proud of you," she said, and let go of the lid. He started to reply, but the pod sealed shut and she couldn't hear him.

There was a rattling behind her. A tarantula landed on the walkway, its sharp metal legs click-clacking as it prepared to pounce. She kicked it aside and it tumbled over the edge into the gravity well and vanished. More spider bots appeared above her, scuttling upside down as they clattered over the sealed drop pods that lined the walls. Their pincers snapped at her menacingly.

Casey dived into the next empty pod. A harness zipped around her body, holding her in place, and the door slid shut. Just as the pod closed, three tarantulas landed on the top and scurried onto the viewing window. Their sleek underbellies and pincers were centimetres from her face. She turned her head away in fright. The tarantulas pinched and jabbed at the glass. She prayed it was thick enough to hold them back.

At the same moment, an Arcturian voice delivered a recorded announcement that was streamed into the pods. Although she didn't recognize the alien words, she'd played enough games of *SkyWake* to know exactly what they were saying. It was the launch countdown timer.

*Preparing drop pod launch. On my mark: five …
four … three … two … one … DROP!*

She felt a shudder as the doors at the bottom of the gravity well opened and then, with a jolt, the drop pods began to tumble out of it. The tarantulas on the viewing window were ripped off the pod and sucked into space. Casey's pod fell from the rack, following the others, and plummeted straight out of the belly of the dropship. She looked up through the viewing window as she left the ship, seeing the huge Arcturian vessel above her and the hundreds of drop pods flying out of it like bees from a hive.

Instinctively, she reached for the dog tags around her neck. Then she remembered, with a jolt, that they weren't there any more.

30

HOT DROP

The drop pod streaked through space. Casey, strapped inside its narrow compartment, felt like she was in a blender. She held on to her harness as she was buffeted from side to side. There was a shudder as the pod pierced the atmosphere of the planet below. She felt the temperature rising beneath her feet as the pod's metal casing began to heat up. Flames burst around the bottom of it and lapped its side viewing windows. For a terrifying moment, she thought she was going to be cooked alive.

A digital display screen in front of her face flashed whirring alien warning symbols. She guessed it was some kind of altimeter, counting down the distance between the pod and the ground. The surface of the planet was coming up fast.

We're almost there, Casey told herself. *Just hold*

it together a little longer. The pod's computerized navigation systems were designed to scan the terrain and lead it from orbit to a safe landing site. She wondered where they'd end up. Would they still be in London? Or might they be jettisoned halfway across the world. Europe, America, maybe even Asia?

She stared out of one of the pod's narrow viewing windows, expecting to see the familiar and comforting green and blue disc of the Earth, the one they put in science books about space travel. She'd always wondered what it must be like to be an astronaut in orbit looking down on the planet she called home.

She gasped.

The planet below her wasn't home at all.

It was blue and watery like Earth but its continents were strange and unfamiliar. Beyond the planet's horizon sat two alien suns – one big and pink, one smaller and redder – set against a backdrop of endless stars.

"Hosin?" Casey whispered, unable to believe her eyes.

Her stomach flipped in terror. She'd imagined the dropship hovering in orbit somewhere above the Earth. How stupid she was not to have realized that the Red Eyes had no need to wait around. They'd got what they'd come for. Why wouldn't they rush to Hosin and send their new troops into the never-ending battle there?

The dropship, travelling faster than light, must have made the journey while they were fighting the Red Eyes in the loadout bay. She remembered the tremor they'd felt and cursed herself. How could she have been so stupid? And, more importantly, how would they ever get home?

The pods were in the air above the planet now. They fell towards a craggy shoreline that stretched for miles, twisting and turning back in on itself as it curved away into the distance. She recognized the shore instantly; knew this beach...

This was the level she'd played over and over again in *SkyWake*. Her favourite. The one she knew best of all. This was what the game had trained them for. They were going to fight the Squids for real.

KABOOM!

The pod shuddered as a plasma shell exploded in the air beside it. A jagged piece of shell casing pierced the side of the pod, stopping just centimetres away from Casey's leg. She willed the pod to hurry its descent, desperate to get out before it became her coffin. If she was going to die, she wanted to die on the beach, standing in the fresh air.

As panic tightened her chest, she wondered how the others were doing. Through the viewing window she could see hundreds of pods dropping like black stones through the sky around her. She prayed her brother and her friends would make it down in one piece. She thought of Elite – would he be freaking out trapped inside this—

KABOOM! Another shell exploded, rocking her pod. She was close enough now to see figures and vehicles moving on the purple-tinged sand below. From this height, they were like toy figures on a tabletop battlefield.

For a moment, she thought the beach was on fire. Then she realized that what she was seeing was the plasma fire of hundreds of troops as they pushed up the shore, charging towards the Squids' defensive positions in the cliffs at the top of the beach. Red Eye attack craft streaked through the sky, engines roaring as they swooped and pitched and then unleashed their weapons at the Squids' bunkers. Explosions burst in the air around them as the enemy retaliated, raining plasma fire on the advancing gamers and their Red Eye commanders.

An alarm screeched inside her drop pod as the

glyphs on the altimeter spiralled out of control. With just seconds to go, Casey realized that she needed to brace for impact. The ground was about to—

Ker-unch!

The drop pod slammed into the purple-tinged sand, embedding itself in the beach. Casey yelled as she was jolted around inside it like a rag doll. The pod's circuits sparked and smoked and then blew out.

After the frantic speed and screaming alarms of the journey down to Hosin, the silent hush that now descended was strange and eerie. Casey felt dazed, uncertain what to do next.

Before she could panic, the pod cracked open. It fell apart in segments like a tapped Chocolate Orange. As its metal casing thudded into the sand, Casey's harness automatically unclipped and snapped away from her chest. The servomotors on her exo-suit whirred as she stepped out onto the sand.

It was the noise that hit her first.

Hundreds of rifles, rockets and fighter jets combined to create a wall of sound. Stepping into it was like being punched in the head. She could barely think straight. Columns of black smoke from a couple of wrecked Red Eye attack ships billowed into the sky, twisting and turning in the wind like tornadoes. She took a step forwards and then another, instinctively aware from her hours of playing *SkyWake* that she needed to keep moving.

Her visor flickered as streams of information flowed over it. A mini-map showed her objective, a red waypoint at the very top of the beach. Casey gripped her plasma rifle and pressed on, looking for her friends.

She quickly found herself flanked by dozens of gamer-soldiers, all wearing exo-suits just like hers. She saw Xander among them. He pushed past her, marching up the beach blank-faced and emotionless. If he recognized her, he showed no sign.

"Xander!" she shouted. She grabbed his arm, trying to shake some sense into him. But he didn't even acknowledge her presence and merely pulled away. "What's wrong with you?" she cried, pulling him back. As she did, his helmet slid backwards to reveal the wire mesh spread over his head. It flickered with flashing LEDs.

Xander pulled away from her a second time and righted his helmet before marching into the Squids' incessant artillery fire. His face was emotionless and impassive, like that of a man possessed. The rest of the Strike Force clan waited for him to catch up. Then they advanced up the beach as a squad. It was as if they were under some kind of remote control.

Casey was about to go after them when she heard a shout off to her left. A few metres across the beach she spotted Pete and the Ghost Reapers stumbling out of their drop pods. There was no sign of Dreyfus. She went to join them.

The boys stared, open-mouthed, at the chaos around them.

"I'm dreaming, right?" Elite muttered. "Gotta be dreaming."

A Red Eye overseer came over and shoved them forwards, shouting something incomprehensible in his alien tongue. Casey didn't need a translator to know he was telling them to move.

That was what you did on the beach. You kept moving or you died.

"Come on," Casey said. She grabbed her brother, keenly aware that he wasn't wearing combat armour. The rest of her team fanned out behind her across the sand. They all ducked as a plasma shell whooshed over their heads and landed behind them, right where they'd just been standing. The abandoned drop pods and the overseer vanished in the explosion.

"What do we do now?" Fish asked, activating his energy shield.

Casey looked around at the beach. "The only thing we can do," she said. "We fight. On me, everyone."

The boys fell into formation, Fish up front with his shield, the others taking cover behind him. They had done this a million times before back at home, sitting in front of their monitors. Now they were here for real.

Casey clutched her plasma rifle as more artillery shells exploded around them, throwing sand and dirt into the air. She led her team forwards.

Today was going to get a whole lot worse before it got better.

Acknowledgements

Writing a book can feel like a lonely journey into the final frontier, but I am lucky to have a brilliant crew on the bridge with me. *SkyWake* would never have seen the light of day without the tireless love and encouragement of my wife, Louise, and daughters, Isobel and Alice. They read the first few chapters and convinced me to keep going, sustaining me throughout with love and laughter. Like pretty much everything else in my life, I couldn't have done it without them.

A big thank you to the rest of my family – Mum, Dad and Lorna – for all their love and support, not to mention the purchase of various home computers and consoles back in the prehistoric, pre-internet days. See? All those years spent blasting aliens and collecting coins was research! Thanks too to John and Anna-Maria Groombridge for many past kindnesses.

I am lucky to have not one but two amazing agents. Andrew Mills at JAB Management has been a rock during my years as a stuck-in-development screenwriter. Meanwhile, Ella Kahn at DKW Literary Agency is a bona fide superhero. Her ability to switch between offering a steely-eyed overview of the market to giving keen notes on structure and character is incredible.

When I drew up a tentative list of my dream publishers, it's no exaggeration to say that Walker Books was right at the top. My family has worked its way through their entire catalogue, from pre-school bear hunts to middle grade super-spies and YA vampires. I am supremely grateful to Denise Johnstone-Burt, Emma Lidbury and Gráinne Clear for championing Casey and for being such utterly wonderful people to work with. A big shout-out to Megan Quibell for her sensitivity read, Margaret Hope for her fantastic art design and Kirsten Cozens and John Moore for all their super publicity work. And a huge thank you to everyone else at Walker Books who's been part of bringing *SkyWake* to life behind the scenes in secret ways I don't even know about. You're all amazing publishing ninjas, each and every one of you.

Thanks also to the super-talented Matt Griffin for his brilliant cover art; the super-lovely Liz Hyder for all her generous cheerleading; Nerdy Coffee Co. in Shrewsbury for boardgames, vegan cakes and general awesomeness; and the 2021 debut authors community (especially the crew of the MG/YA Good Ship collective for all the support and laughs).

Finally, thank you to you … the reader. Writing a novel and putting it in someone's hands is nerve-racking, but it's also a real privilege. So thank you for picking up this book. I hope you enjoy reading it as much as I did writing it.

And remember: go with the flow…

Jamie Russell is a former contributing editor of *Total Film* magazine turned screenwriter and author. He has written several non-fiction books, including *Book of the Dead: The Complete History of Zombie Cinema* and *Generation Xbox: How Videogames Invaded Hollywood*. *SkyWake: Invasion* is the first in a planned trilogy and is Jamie's first book for children.